Mariah Delany's Author-of-the-Month Club

Mariah Delany's Author-of-the-Month Club

SHEILA GREENWALD

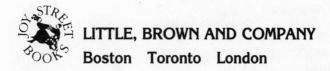

JOY STREET BOOKS

LITTLE, BROWN AND COMPANY
Boston   Toronto   London

First edition

The characters and events in this book are fictitious. Any
similarity to real persons, living or dead, is coincidental
and not intended by the author.

Library of Congress Cataloging-in-Publication Data

Greenwald, Sheila.
   Mariah Delany's author-of-the-month club / by Sheila
Greenwald. — 1st ed.
      p.   cm.
   Summary: Mariah invites authors to speak at her
Author-of-the-Month Club with near disastrous results.
   ISBN 0-316-32713-1
   [1. Authors — Fiction. 2. Humorous stories.]   I. Title.
PZ7.G852Marb   1990
[Fic] — dc20   89-49508
                                                       CIP
                                                        AC

Joy Street Books are published by
Little, Brown and Company (Inc.)

10 9 8 7 6 5 4 3 2 1
BP
Published simultaneously in Canada
by Little, Brown & Company (Canada) Limited

Printed in the United States of America

Mariah Delany's Author-of-the-Month Club

1

Mariah Delany, you have that look again," her mother remarked at breakfast one morning.

"What look?"

"The sort of look you get before you decide to start a chain of lemonade stands or teach harmonica or sell plants out of the building lobby. The sort of look you got when you opened that Lending Library."

"What sort of look?" Mariah asked again, hoping for a more specific description. It made her uncomfortable to think that her thoughts could be read on her face without her knowing it.

"Narrowed eyes, thin lips," Mrs. Delany summed up.

Mariah quickly opened her green eyes as wide as possible and relaxed her small mouth as best she could. "I was just wondering about books," she said.

"Books?" Mrs. Delaney smiled happily. Books to the Delanys were like nuts to a family of squirrels. They couldn't live without them. Books were everywhere in the apartment. They rose in stacks from the floor. They crammed every inch of shelf space, which lined every foot of wall space that was not taken up by a window or a door. They toppled from the tabletops and on occasion had even taken over the ironing board and the piano bench. Mariah's mother was a professor of English and her father a publisher of books. Her brother, Irwin, took his face out of one only long enough to lower it to a plate of food. It was only Mariah who had a practical turn of mind. Unfortunately, that led to schemes her parents never understood, much less approved of.

"What about books?" Mrs. Delany asked.

"The people who write them."

"Authors, you mean?"

"Authors, yes. We had one visit school."

"How nice." Mrs. Delany looked at the clock.

Mariah was relieved to see that her mother was no longer interested in observing her narrowed eyes and thin lips, but was thinking of her

4

own eight-forty-five class at City University. She watched her mother stack her mug and plate, dust off her lapels, and stand up to deposit the dirty dishes in the dishwasher. "We'll discuss authors tonight at dinner." She kissed Mariah distractedly on the top of her head. "Please remind me."

Mariah finished her milk and the rest of her bagel and set her dishes beside her mother's in the machine. It was time for school. More to the point, it was time to consult with some old friends on her new brainstorm.

It had all started yesterday with the special guest assembly at school. The special guest was Janice Pike, author of the twelve Willy Wild books. Mariah and all her classmates had read them, not only because they were on the list of the Reading-Is-Fun Book Club, which the whole class subscribed to, but because they were funny and interesting and short. Willy Wild had hilarious adventures and got into awful scrapes that he always managed to get out of at the last minute in some surprising way. The biggest surprise about Willy Wild, however, turned out to be Janice Pike.

Mariah had never given "J. Pike" (as it was written on the covers of the books) a thought, much less imagined that the books were written by a redheaded woman who was as funny and interesting and almost as short as Willy Wild himself. "I never run out of adventures for Willy," she confided. "All I have to do is think back to when my brothers and I were growing up in Chicago." She leaned toward them as if she were about to share a secret. "I'll tell you an adventure. I may use it for Willy." She winked at them. "If I don't use it for Willy, it will be just for you."

To be one of the few people on earth who knew an adventure Willy Wild might or might not have made Mariah feel excited and happy all at once. It was like receiving a special present.

Standing on line after Janice Pike's talk to have her own Willy Wild book signed by the author, Mariah could tell that her classmates felt the way she did.

Emma Pinkwater was jumping up and down. "What a thrill to actually meet the person who actually wrote the book and know that any minute now she will put her name in my very own copy."

"Maybe she'll write something personal in my book," Dave Peterson said. "People tell me I look like Willy."

Mariah examined Dave with new interest. She had always thought he looked like trouble, but now that he mentioned it he did bear a resemblance to Willy, whose "straw-colored hair stood up in unexpected places."

When it was Mariah's turn to present her book, Janice Pike glanced up and smiled. "What's your name?" she asked.

"Mariah Delany," Mariah said.

"I've always been partial to the name Mariah," Janice Pike said. "Maybe one day I'll borrow it for one of my characters." She scribbled her own name into Mariah's copy and closed it. "I see you got this copy through the book club. Aren't book clubs a wonderful idea?"

"Oh, yes," Mariah agreed. Being a member of the book club meant that every month she could pick out a book from the list the club offered and buy it for only a dollar and a half. The books were delivered to club members' classrooms a few weeks after the orders had been placed.

Janice Pike's words stuck in Mariah's mind for the rest of the day. Even after school, walking home with Emma Pinkwater, Suzy Bellamy, and Leah Coopersmith, she thought of the words "Aren't book clubs a wonderful idea?"

Emma held her book up over her head. "I'm going to put this on the shelf where my family keeps really valuable things. I just can't believe I met a real live author."

"Neither can I," Leah agreed. "I wish we could have an author for every assembly."

"I wish we could have authors come the way the books do," Emma said. "Once a month."

"We could have," Mariah said, thinking out loud. "We could have a club that would bring them to us," she said, getting excited. A club that would provide a real live author like Janice Pike to come and talk to its members once a month. A club that delivered authors the way the Reading-Is-Fun Book Club delivered books. At this point Mariah's nose began to quiver. It always did when she was about to come up with a sensational new idea. Some people loved reading books. Some people loved meeting authors. But more than anything, Mariah loved making things happen. She knew how to do it; she had a talent for knowing what the public wanted and getting it to them. Lemonade on a hot day, a Lending Library when the Public Library's hours were cut back. This was the instinct of a true businessperson. Sometimes she had unforeseen problems, but her new idea seemed like a hands-down winner. And she knew just what to call it.

The Mariah Delany Author-of-the-Month Club.

2

I don't see how we can get the authors to accept," Leah Coopersmith said. "I know for a fact that the Parents' Association raised money to pay Janice Pike. They even paid for her lunch. How can we afford writers, and where will you have them talk and autograph books?"

"Every month there will be a meeting at my place," Mariah said quickly, as if it were obvious. She knew her parents would be more than happy to offer their living room for her great idea. After all, they were both eager to promote reading whenever they could. "If each club member pays the price of a Reading-Is-Fun Book, we can raise almost twenty-five dollars," Mariah said, glad she had worked this out beforehand.

"I know for a fact that Janice Pike got three hundred dollars from the P.A.," Leah said, "and that was a bargain."

"Three hundred?" Mariah was not prepared for this. "How come you know everything for a fact?" she grumbled.

"My mother is head of the Student Enrichment Program," Leah said coolly.

"What's that supposed to mean?" Emma took her long face out of the tumbler of hot cocoa that had absorbed all her attention. Hot cocoa was a specialty of the Coopersmith household. Whenever the friends gathered at Leah's after school, they headed straight for the kitchen.

"It means that meeting Janice Pike has made us richer," Leah explained.

"I guess there are two kinds of being rich," Mariah acknowledged bleakly. Unless she could come up with the one having to do with dollars, she would have to forget about the one having to do with authors.

"We could raise money from parents," Emma suggested. "They might like the idea."

"I'm not so sure," Suzy said. "My mom told Mrs. Ludlow that if she gave to one more whale, she'd be harpooned for not paying the rent."

Mariah didn't know about Mrs. Bellamy or the whales, but Suzy had just sent a harpoon sailing through her brainstorm.

"Your idea is interesting," Leah said without looking at Mariah. "I'm just not sure it can work."

"Not sure it can work?" Mariah repeated, turning to Emma for encouragement.

"You know me," Emma said, squirming. "I'm shy. I don't know anything about tracking down writers and inviting them."

10

"I'm no joiner," Suzy said bluntly. "I don't like clubs."

Mariah searched each of their faces one by one. Emma was shy, Suzy was "no joiner," and even Leah, whom she could usually count on for enthusiastic help, still wasn't looking at her. Why weren't they jumping out of their seats, pleading to be part of her plan? Here she was, offering to see to it that they would have J. Pike–like authors sign their books and tell them wonderful, never-before-known, inside-track, straight-poop book information. Her club would bring them the stories behind the stories and the characters behind the characters. On a Regular Basis. No Strings Attached. If she were an investment adviser, she'd sell it like a blue-chip stock, for heaven's sake. Why couldn't they see it?

"Dave Peterson is still furious with me for the way we made him return his book to the Lending Library," Emma mumbled.

"It wasn't his book," Mariah snapped, "and he was never going to return it. He was about to give it to his mother for a gift. I wouldn't care if he never talked to me again." But in fact she did care. Everybody liked Dave Peterson. Perhaps if she could sign him up for her club, timid friends like Emma might follow.

"More cocoa?" Leah held up the pot.

Mariah stood and gathered her knapsack and jacket. The cocoa was good, but she had important things on her mind. She had to think up some way to start her club without her friends. She had to find an author . . . for free.

All the way home Mariah turned the problem over in her head. She didn't feel the rough wind that blew so hard against her she could practically lean on it. She didn't even notice Josie Levine tearing down the street after her. Josie lived two floors below her in the same building and was always trying to get in on Mariah's projects. After the plant sale, Mariah didn't entirely trust her.

"I'm so sorry I went ahead and sold plants in the lobby without you," Josie apologized for the twentieth time. "I hope that doesn't mean you won't include me in any of your future plans."

"It does," Mariah said.

"Why?" Josie wailed. "You included me in the plant sale."

"That was because you had plants. You couldn't help me now even if I wanted you to."

"What do you need now?" Josie asked timidly.

"A writer," Mariah said.

Josie's face broke into a radiant smile. "But I *can* help you," she said.

They had just arrived in the lobby of their building and were both a bit dazed by the blast of heat that hissed from its radiators. "I just finished a short story and I'm starting a poem," Josie said slowly. "I am a writer."

"I need a real professional writer like Janice Pike who will come and discuss her work. A writer people have heard of and read."

"One day I'll be a writer people have heard of and read," Josie insisted. "It just hasn't happened yet."

"How can you be so sure?" Mariah pressed the elevator button and viewed Josie Levine with new interest. After calling herself a writer, Josie was standing up a bit straighter and holding her head at a more confident tilt.

"My mother tells me I'm a writer," Josie answered. "And my mother ought to know. She's Features Editor of *Woman's Horizon* magazine."

As far as Mariah had known, Josie's mother was a slender woman with a bulging briefcase and running shoes who was always in a hurry and had once lost a contact lens in the lobby. What was Features Editor of *Woman's Horizon* magazine?

"Would you care to hear me do a reading?" Josie asked as the elevator opened at her floor.

Mariah stepped out behind her.

Josie's apartment had the same layout as the Delanys', but walls had been knocked down to create large white spaces with hardly any furniture in them. A low sofa and a few oriental screens made up the living room. Where the Delanys had books, the Levines had plants. Spider plants hung in baskets, dieffenbachia and Christmas cactus

13

and jade plants vied for space on windowsills and mantels. Mariah remembered something. It was her Independent Science Project, "Observing Plant Life," which she had not begun.

"Could you spare me a small plant?" she asked.

Josie selected a potted begonia and sneezed. "I think I'm allergic to them."

Mariah sympathized. The sight of the plant and the thought of her project made her feel a little sick, too.

In Josie's room the plants gave way to stuffed animals.

"Clear a space and sit down." Josie pointed to the mass of plush ducks, under which Mariah assumed there was a bed. On the floor sticking out from under the bed was a pair of shiny patent leather shoes with taps on them. "Those are my tap shoes," Josie said proudly. "Tap is my other talent. I even have a little portable dance floor to practice on." She removed her jacket and dropped her book bag on a small desk, from which she took a bound black book with a label on its cover. "My Works on Paper," it read. Carefully she opened the volume and cleared her throat. "This is a story about Marianna Appleby, who lived in a faraway country that was an island." She spoke in an unfamiliar, singsong, stuffed-nose voice.

Mariah shoved a bunch of ducks aside and, holding the begonia on her lap, sat down to listen. But it was hard to listen. The singsong voice and funny

swaying motion of Josie's body sent Mariah's
thoughts off on a track of their own. She pictured
her first meeting. She could imagine the rows of
folding chairs arranged in the living room, form-
ing a semicircle around Josie Levine. She imagined her club members sitting in an entranced
state of delight, listening to Josie's singsong story.
In spite of her runny nose, Josie read with the
confidence of a real published author. Clearly, all
she needed was time and luck (like the club) to be
a success. Maybe it would be a good idea to start
the club off with an undiscovered writer, Mariah
decided, especially one who would read for free.

"How would you like to read your work to a
group of people and then discuss it and answer
questions about it?" Mariah said, interrupting
Josie.

"You mean the way Janice Pike did in assembly?
I would love that!" Josie gasped. "Then everybody

in my class would know that I am not Josie the doof, but Josie the writer."

"Wait a minute." Mariah shook her head. "I plan to keep your identity a secret. You will be a mystery writer."

"But I don't write mysteries."

"*You'll* be the mystery."

"Then *nobody will* know that it's me." Josie stopped smiling.

"It will be better that way," Mariah said, not wanting to explain that with Josie billed as the writer, there wouldn't be an audience. "We'll keep them in suspense. We'll tell them your name at the second meeting. That way we'll get them to come back."

"But they'll know it's me when I stand up to read."

Mariah squinted at Josie and thought about this. "Maybe it would be a good idea to dress you up."

"Put me in disguise?" Josie was alarmed.

"Nothing much," Mariah reassured her. "A big hat, dark glasses, a wig maybe."

"What about my name? Joanna Doris Levine."

"How about J.D?" Mariah suggested. "It sounds like a writer. J.D."

"J.D.?" Josie tried it out.

"Think about it," Mariah said. "We have time."

"No we don't!" Josie cried. "I need a reading. I'm J.D. I'm ready."

This was fine with Mariah. She had been without

16

a project long enough. She couldn't wait for the hustle and bustle of signing up members, collecting dues, and assigning jobs. She couldn't wait to be back in business.

"We'll hold our first meeting of the Mariah Delany Author-of-the-Month Club on the Wednesday before spring vacation," she told Josie. "That gives us two weeks."

3

What's that poster for?" Dave Peterson asked
Mariah as she tacked it up on the third-floor
bulletin board.

"Join my club and you'll find out." She smiled
warmly, hoping that Dave would and everyone
else would follow.

"I didn't think you'd want me after what I did
with your father's copy of *Great Expectations*."

"Oh, that." Mariah waved her hand as if it didn't
matter at all. "What did you do anyway? Borrow
my father's first edition of *Great Expectations* from
my Lending Library and try to give it to your
mother for an anniversary present. Big deal."

"I didn't know it was that valuable," Dave said
miserably.

"Neither did I," Mariah confessed for the first
time. "I borrowed the book from my father without telling him I was using it for my Lending Library, and you borrowed it from my Lending
Library without telling me you were going to give
it to your parents."

"You mean we both made a mistake?" Dave asked hopefully.

"Maybe." Mariah nodded.

"So how can I help you now?" Dave asked. He seemed so grateful to Mariah to be let off the hook, he would do anything.

"Posters." She pointed to the one she had just hung. "Phone calls, getting the word out. Everybody likes you, Dave. You'd be good at that."

"They do? I would?" He flushed with pleasure and surprise and reached for the posters she still carried under her arm. "I could get those up for you," he offered.

Mariah handed him all the ones she had. "Tell as many people as you can about our first meeting and the appearance of the Mystery Author," she said as she turned into the locker room.

Mariah found Emma and Leah and Suzy packing up their knapsacks and zipping their jackets.

"*Dave* believes in my club," she called out breathlessly.

"It isn't that I don't believe in your club," Leah said. "It's just that I don't believe other people are ready for it."

"It's not only having a good idea," Suzy added. "It's making it work."

"To make my idea work, I need help," Mariah said.

"What kind of help?" Leah asked guiltily.

"I need someone whose mother has a copying

machine to make up fliers and notices about my meeting."

"I've got the mother with the copying machine." Leah slumped in a resigned way and reached for her notepad. "What should the fliers say?"

"First meeting of the Author-of-the-Month Club. Come meet the Mystery Writer."

"You've got Nancy Drew?" Emma screamed.

"Nancy Drew is just a character in mystery books," Mariah scoffed. "*My* writer *is* the mystery. You won't know who she is."

"Is she in the library?" Suzy asked.

"Sometimes." Mariah looked vague. "You'll only find out her identity at the second meeting of the Author-of-the-Month Club."

Leah closed her pad. "I've got enough for a flier."

"Are there going to be free refreshments?" Suzy wanted to know.

"If someone donates them." Mariah glared at Emma.

"I'll donate them." Emma sighed.

"Make them Oreos, and I'll be there," Suzy told her.

Mariah could see that things were looking up. She had someone to do fliers, someone to do posters, someone to buy cookies, and someone to eat them. She felt so good, she nearly forgot her biggest worry, the someone who would be author. At four o'clock that afternoon she had an appointment with J.D. to prepare her for her debut.

At exactly four o'clock Josie appeared at Mariah's door. She had her bound volume under one arm and a folder marked "Unfinished Work" in her hand. She wore a long velvet skirt over blue jeans, dark glasses, and a velour hat with a wide brim. "This puts me in the mood," she explained.

"Perfect," Mariah said approvingly. Without realizing it, Josie had put herself in disguise as well. "All you need now is a little makeup and a wig."

"I don't know about that." Josie pulled on her thin brown hair. "It might not feel right."

Mariah took Josie into her mother's room, where she applied some old caked rouge to Josie's pale cheeks. Then she led her back to the living room and positioned her in the curve of the piano, as if she were a singer.

"Once there was a girl named Marianna Appleby," Josie began to croon, "whose mother told her not to touch her box of bubble-bath beads."

Mariah could imagine Josie, in her funny hat and long skirt, swaying slightly to the rhythm of her high-pitched, singsong voice, as a twenty-six-year-old professional writer. A writer who had been given her start by the Mariah Delany Author-of-the-Month Club. Once again the singsong voice sent Mariah's thoughts wandering to club business. She would set up a small folding table by the door on the day of the meeting so that new members could line up and sign up before they left. She could just see herself seated at the table, registering all the new club members on individual file cards and handing out membership cards. It was such a wonderful scene that it wasn't until Josie's voice suddenly stopped that she realized the sound she heard in its place was the doorbell.

It was Mrs. Levine. "Is my daughter here?" she demanded in the same panicked tone of voice Mariah heard from her own mother when she had forgotten to leave word where she would be.

Mariah didn't have to answer, because Josie was just behind her.

"Joanna, you've given me a scare!" her mother exclaimed. "Why didn't you leave a note? It's a good thing the doorman suggested you might be at Mariah's." She paused and noticed Josie's getup. "What on earth are you doing in my skirt and hat, with all that stuff on your face?"

"It's a secret." Josie pouted, eyeing Mariah.

"You can tell your mother," Mariah said. "Josie's the first author to appear at my Author-of-the-Month Club meeting. We want to keep her identity a secret until the second meeting."

"Why?" Mrs. Levine protested. "She shouldn't be a secret."

"It's because I'm the Mystery Author, J.D.," Josie said, standing up for Mariah's argument, much to Mariah's relief.

"Can the Mystery Author's mother take pictures of her reading?" Mrs. Levine asked.

Picture taking could be a tipoff to Josie's identity, Mariah thought, but it could also lend an element of excitement and glamour. She didn't think any of her classmates would recognize Mrs. Levine. "You can take pictures of the meeting," she said.

"Thank you, Mariah." Mrs. Levine grinned. "I'm so eager to come, *I'd* even wear a disguise in order to be there."

The next morning Mariah felt like leaping out of bed. Even her usual breakfast of toasted sesame bagel and steamed milk with cinnamon tasted better. When she got to school, it was just as she'd hoped. Everyone in her class had seen the posters and was interested in coming to the first meeting of the Author-of-the-Month Club. They liked the fact that dues were only a quarter (to cover paper for publicity and posters) and that refreshments were free.

"You've done a great job," Mariah congratulated Dave. His red-and-white posters were all over the school.

"Hanging posters isn't everything," Leah said. "What about my fliers?"

Mariah had hoped to avoid this question. She also wanted to avoid rereading the flier. It made her wonder if Leah was really a friend.

ANOTHER IDEA FROM THE PERSON WHO
BROUGHT YOU THE MARIAH DELANY
LENDING LIBRARY HA HA HA
COME ONE COME ALL
MEET THE MYSTERY WRITER YOU
ALWAYS WANTED TO KNOW??????

"What are all those question marks and the 'ha ha ha' for?" Mariah asked.

"The Lending Library was a disaster," Leah explained, "and how can we always want to know somebody if we don't know who they are?"

"Come to my meeting and you'll find out," Mariah promised. Clearly, she still had to do some convincing of her supporters, but she knew that once they came to the first meeting, they'd see the light.

4

Before Mariah knew it, it was the Wednesday morning before spring vacation. She went into the kitchen, put her bagel in the toaster oven, and crossed her fingers. "I'm holding the first meeting of my Author-of-the-Month Club at four o'clock this afternoon," she informed her parents, who were sitting behind her at the breakfast table.

"The first meeting of the WHAT?" Mrs. Delany came out from behind her newspaper.

"Author-of-the-Month Club." Mr. Delany came out from behind his magazine. "Hers."

"This is very short notice, Mariah," Mrs. Delany said.

"I did mention it a few weeks ago," Mariah reminded her. "I thought it would be all right."

"I do remember something," Mrs. Delany said. "This must be that idea I asked you to remind me about later."

"Is this anything like that Lending Library?" her

25

father asked. "Or those lemonade stands and harmonica lessons?"

"Oh, no!" Mariah exclaimed. "It's just a way to meet real live authors whose books we love."

Mrs. Delany seemed puzzled. "Since it's the books you love, why do you have to meet the authors?"

Mariah was speechless! Once again, her mother had totally failed to comprehend one of her brainstorms. "What about T. M. Obermeyer?"

Mrs. Delany closed her eyes and smiled blissfully, as she always did at the mention of the author of all five Fanny Frost books. "I have no desire to know if T. M. Obermeyer is a man or a woman, dead or alive. I have loved those books since I was a girl. The books are what's important."

"Man or woman, dead or alive. . . . The Authorof-the-Month Club sounds like a harmless enough idea," Mr. Delany said. "I don't see what trouble can come of it."

Mrs. Delany hesitated. "I just hope Mariah isn't biting off more than she can chew again. I'll leave a note for Teresa."

Teresa Todd was the housekeeper, who tried to make order around the stacks of books in the Delany apartment once a week. She and Mariah sympathized with each other for having to put up with them. But even if she had her doubts about books, Mrs. Todd loved clubs. She belonged to several herself. They had to do with Bingo, Clog Dancing, and Low Blood Sugar. Mariah had already mentioned the club to Mrs. Todd, and together they had counted out the folding chairs and the number of spots that could be used for seating in the living room.

Mariah was grateful that there was so much preparation for her meeting (arranging trays of juice in small paper cups, getting plates for the Oreos, setting up chairs in rows, coaxing Josie into makeup and wig, reviewing her introduction), since it took her mind off her main worry: keeping J.D.'s identity a secret. But by three-thirty that afternoon, with the chairs all in place, the cookies and juice cups arranged like a little army on two trays, and J.D. behind dark glasses, wig, hat, rouge, and sweeping skirt posing for her mother's camera, Mariah's worries were forgotten. Everything looked fine.

By ten minutes of four, the doorbell began to go off so regularly that she finally left the door ajar. In fifteen minutes every seat in the living room had been taken. Mrs. Todd and Emma were passing the last of the refreshments, and Mariah was standing by the piano and calling for quiet.

"Welcome to the first meeting of the Author-of-the-Month Club," she began. "Every month this exciting new club will bring you a famous writer whose books you know and love. Sometimes, for the fun of it, we will bring you a famous author you don't know and love yet, but whose books you

27

would love if you got a chance. Today, our author is an exciting new talent. You can say you were the very first to discover her. You don't know her now, but once you've heard her read, you'll never forget her. Here she is: J.D."

J.D. swayed a little, as if she were accepting a standing ovation, when actually there had only been some light hand clapping.

"This work is called *Marianna Appleby*," she began in her weird singsong, I'm-reading-to-you voice. Mrs. Levine started clicking away, taking pictures of the audience and of Josie from every angle.

Mariah stood at the back of the room and observed. At first everyone leaned forward to catch every word. They even chewed cookies with their mouths closed or stopped chewing completely. Mariah tried to listen, too, but soon the story began to drift and wander like a bubble. It bobbed here and there. It was impossible to follow. Mariah's heart sank. She realized she had never really listened before! She was always too busy planning the meeting, perfecting Josie's disguise, or thinking about how to arrange the chairs. She noticed Eric Berson nudge Helena Murty and whisper in her ear. Then Helena nudged Herbie Lustig and whispered and Herbie nudged Suzy Bellamy. Something was happening that was even worse than Josie's story! Mariah had to stop it before it was too late.

Suddenly Eric Berson's hand waved in the air. "Wait a minute!" he yelped. "That's Josie Levine!"

It *was* too late.

Josie stopped reading.

"It's Josie Levine in a hat and a wig and dark glasses," Suzy added.

Everybody began to laugh.

Josie took off the glasses and the hat and bowed deeply.

"Hey, Josie, how does it feel to be a famous author?"

"It was a real pain when I had to conceal my identity." She glared at Mariah.

"That's some story. Where do you get your ideas?"

"The bathtub."

"The bathtub?" A few people laughed.

"Glub-glub. This story is drowning me," someone else said.

A number of people pretended to be drowning, while others pretended to be scrubbing themselves.

"Say, Mariah, can I be your next famous author of the month?" Helena Murty hollered over the din. "I get my ideas in the shower, so they're a little wet, too, but I'lll dry them out for the meeting."

"Next month we'll have a known author," Mariah said quickly, hurrying up to the front of the room.

"Who's that?" Eric demanded. "Rubber Ducky?"

"Watch the posters," Mariah answered, looking pleadingly at Dave.

"That's right!" Dave bellowed. "Look for my posters. They'll tell you about the next meeting. It will top anything you could dream of."

"You mean Josie Levine?" someone said, laughing.

"Josie Levine is hard to top," Mrs. Levine called out in a cracked angry voice that Mariah worried might turn into a cry.

"That's right. I am," Josie said defiantly. Mariah couldn't believe her courage in the face of extreme teasing.

Mariah never set up her table by the door. There was no need to. No one was standing on line to sign up for the club.

Josie strutted past, holding up her skirt. "Even though they didn't understand what I was trying to do, at least they know I'm a writer now. Next time I could read again as a KNOWN."

"You can keep the leftover cookies," Emma whispered to Mariah. "They'll make you feel better."

"I'm sorry it worked out this way," Suzy said. "I won't say I told you so. I wouldn't rub it in."

"Should I stay for a while?" Leah asked.

Mariah shook her head. She couldn't wait for them all to clear out. When they were gone, she closed the door and leaned against it. The living room was littered with paper cups and folding chairs.

"That seemed like fun," Mrs. Todd said good-heartedly. "Everybody enjoyed themselves. At least this club is no disaster."

"This club isn't a disaster," Mariah agreed. "It's a joke." She began to fold the chairs and stack them in the hall closet. Because tears were beginning to well up, she stayed in the closet for an extra moment. "And the joke was on me."

Mrs. Todd looked puzzled, so Mariah explained about trying to pass Josie off as a real author and her promise to produce one for the next meeting.

"It's a wonderful idea for a club," Mrs. Todd said gently. "But to keep it going, you will have to come up with someone . . . Otherwise . . ."

"Good-bye club," Mariah finished the sentence.

By the time her parents came home from work and Irwin from high school, Mariah was completely miserable. How could her wonderful idea have taken such a nosedive? Where had she gone wrong? It had to be Josie Levine. She needed a real writer. When she told her parents this, Mrs. Delany shook her head.

"That is probably impossible. If I may say so, it's just as well. You have far too much work to do for school to start messing with after-school activities and time-consuming projects. May I remind you of what happened the last time you

31

launched one of these enterprises? The quality of your schoolwork went way down. I don't want to see that happen again. I'm sure you don't either, Mariah. It was VERY UNPLEASANT."

"It won't happen," Mariah said quickly. "I can do both. I promise."

Later in her room, she opened her knapsack and looked at her homework assignment. "Independent Science Project" glared at her from the top of the list. She heaved a sigh and opened the folder Mrs. Demot had given out. "Observing Plant Life" was the general title, but each student had to think up his or her own problem and then (1) Set it up. (2) Assemble material. (3) Chart observations. (4) Draw a conclusion.

Set up a problem? She couldn't think of a single problem other than her club and the fact that everybody else in her class had been hard at work on the science project for a couple of weeks. Suzy was using three different types of soil in three separate pots. Emma was comparing the effect of varying degrees of sunlight on two plants of the same variety. Mariah picked up the little begonia. She had carefully given it a cup of water every third day, as Mrs. Levine had instructed, but it looked terrible. Slowly she wrote the date and the time and "I don't have a problem or material yet, but my observations are (1) The leaves have brownish spots. (2) They droop. (3) My plant looks awful."

"Poor plant." Mariah put it back on the windowsill. She thought of what her mother had said about finding a real author. "It can't be impossible," Mariah told the plant. "There's got to be a way." She was not about to give up before she even started. All the while she got ready for bed, she tried to think of a plan. Finally she lay down and turned off her light. The Author-of-the-Month Club was different from her other enterprises. It wasn't a business. It was to hear stories and think thoughts . . . it would benefit members. That's it! Mariah sat up.

A benefit! She'd organize a benefit to help sponsor the club. Even in the dark she could see it:

AUTHORS FOR KIDS

A BENEFIT

FOR THE . . .

She tried to remember the word the Parents' Association had used. It was . . . "enrichment." Yes, that was it!

FOR THE ENRICHMENT OF

YOUNG READERS

5

Even though it was the beginning of April, the next morning felt as crisp as a fall day, perfect weather, Mariah thought, for a benefit.

Josie was waiting in the lobby of the building with a sequel to *Marianna Appleby*. "I wrote the whole thing last night." She jumped off the lobby bench and scurried after Mariah. "I can read it to you while we walk."

Along with everything else, the Author-of-the-Month Club inspired young authors, Mariah thought. Years from now, Josie would tell the world how the club had given her a start.

"Say" — Josie stopped reading — "you aren't listening."

"I have a lot on my mind," Mariah explained.

"Can I help?"

"We have to figure out how to pay our next author."

"You didn't pay me," Josie reminded her.

"You were the Mystery Author," Mariah said.

"So when do I get paid?" Josie asked.

"That's part of the mystery. But now I need unmysterious cash for an author, and I don't know where to get it."

"I could sell something," Josie said. "I'll sell my ducks."

"I wouldn't ask you to do that."

"It's okay. My doctor thinks I'm allergic to the stuffing."

"Well," Mariah said slowly, "if it's for health purposes." She was imagining how the ducks could be the centerpiece for a display of old comics and toys on the sidewalk in front of her building. She could even see the sign in her mind's eye: AUTHORS FOR KIDS, A BENEFIT FLEA MARKET.

"Bring your ducks down to the lobby after school," Mariah said. "Let's see how they fly."

As they approached their school, it was Mariah who wished she could fly, right over the building.

"Glub-glub, here comes the Bubble-Bath Club," someone called to her from across the street.

"I hear five famous writers have asked to talk at your next meeting." Helena Murty leaned across Mariah's desk even before she sat down. "Who will you choose? Emma or Suzy or maybe me?"

"T. M. Obermeyer," Mariah growled, speaking off the top of her head.

"T. M. Obermeyer?" Dave cried from the seat behind her. "That's my mother's favorite writer! I thought he was dead."

"Maybe those are the only authors Mariah can get," Helena teased.

At lunch Mariah chose an empty table at the back of the cafeteria. She sat facing the wall. With luck, no one would join her.

"Is T. M. Obermeyer really your next author?" Emma slid into a chair next to her.

Mariah took a bite of her sandwich and chewed slowly. "Why not?" She shrugged. For a moment she enjoyed a picture of herself introducing T. M. Obermeyer to her astonished club.

"Don't take it so hard," Emma advised. "It's not your fault that this club can't work."

"The Author-of-the-Month Club can work," Mariah insisted.

"If you say so." Emma shook her head as if she were talking to a hopeless case.

"Just wait . . ." Mariah said.

"For when T. M. Obermeyer is your guest?" Emma giggled.

"Maybe. Who knows?"

In the art room, Mariah tried to concentrate on making globs of blue tempera paint resemble a glittering pond. Finally she tore the paper off her pad and took a large piece of oaktag from the rack at the front of the room. She knew what she really wanted to paint. Once she started, she worked quickly until she was done.

AUTHORS FOR KIDS

A BENEFIT TO ENRICH

YOUNG READERS . . . HELP US

PAY AN AUTHOR

"What do you call that?" Mr. Teague, her art teacher, asked.

"A sign," Mariah said.

"But is it art?" Mr. Teague questioned.

"It's art for a good cause." Mariah rolled up the poster even though it was still sticky. She was afraid it would be taken from her if she weren't careful. As soon as class was out, she raced to the locker room, yanked her jacket off its hook, and ran for it.

Reliable Josie was waiting on the lobby bench. In her lap she held a shopping bag full of ducks.

"I'll be right down," Mariah told her, stepping into the elevator.

Up in her own apartment she hastily ransacked her old toy chest. There were things she hadn't looked at for years. Without sorting, she scooped up a bunch of toys, comics, and magazines passed down from Irwin. In minutes her shopping bags were loaded.

On the pavement a few paces from the entrance to their building, Mariah and Josie spread an old blanket and began to arrange their wares. They placed the ducks at the center with the poster propped behind them.

"What do you think?" Josie asked.

Mariah stepped back a few paces. What she thought was that this flea market bore a depressing resemblance to the stacks of neatly packaged trash heaped at the building's service entrance only yards away, awaiting garbage pickup. The ducks looked as it they not only caused allergies but had them. Their eyes were faded and in some cases missing.

"I hate to sell them." Josie picked one up to hug it. "But they'll make us rich."

"Rich?" Mariah began, but she stopped herself. Josie was the only person who believed in her enterprises.

As people rounded the corner from the bus stop, they had to notice the flea market or practically fall over it. Most pretended not to notice. There were tenants going in and out of the building as well as passersby coming from the park. A tenant from 8C who was a friend of Mrs. Levine's purchased a selection of comics. The doorman, Eddie, bought five issues of *Ranger Rick*. A woman asked if she could make an offer on Mariah's mother's blanket.

Mariah thought about it, imagined the expression on her mother's face, and said no.

"Nobody wants my ducks." Josie shook her head in disbelief.

"Nobody understands them," Mariah explained. "Like the club."

A young woman with a knapsack stopped to read the sign. "Authors for kids," she read out loud. "What a terrific idea! You know, you've got an author right here in this building." She pointed to a window on the second floor. "See where those blinds are drawn? Joe Butts lives there."

"Joe Butts?"

"The Outlaw Joe books," the woman said. "He's in the apartment right next to mine. I'll tell him you're here. He'll think this flea market is a hoot."

"A hoot?" Mariah didn't know what this meant. However, she knew she and her friends had all read and liked the Outlaw Joe books. As soon as the woman had disappeared into the lobby, Mariah whipped out her Magic Marker and made an adjustment on the poster:

PAY AUTHOR JOE BUTTS

39

"I don't get it," Josie said.
"Wait," Mariah instructed.

It began to get chilly. The sun was going down.
"I have to go in." Josie shivered. "I have to practice tap dance."
"Tap dance," Mariah scoffed. "A real author is
right there behind that window and we're about
to sign him up and you talk about tap dance." She
remembered that Outlaw Joe was quick on the
trigger and faster on horseback than anybody in
the Montana Territory, but it took five long minutes till Mariah saw him raise the blind on his
second-floor window.
"What's this all about?" he called down gruffly.

"A benefit to raise money for Joe Butts to talk to my Author-of-the-Month Club," Mariah called back quickly.

"Don't go away." The dark bearded face pulled back from the window ledge.

"He looks scary." Josie trembled. "Is this okay?"

When Joe Butts pushed through the building's front door, he did look a bit threatening, but his face was gentle and he seemed amused. "Are you telling me you're raising money to pay ME to talk to your club?"

"If you're Joe Butts," Mariah said. "We would like to hear you discuss your books and answer a few of our questions." She held up the cash box. "But I only have two dollars so far."

"Why didn't you just write me a letter?" Joe Butts asked. "I would have answered."

"But I can't pay you," Mariah repeated.

"I'll talk to your club on the condition that you don't pay me," he said.

"We can do that." Mariah nodded.

"And that every member will have read my books."

"We can do that, too," she said, clutching the cash box to her chest to keep from flinging her arms around him. While Josie packed up the flea market, Mariah and Joe Butts settled on Wednesday after spring vacation as the time for the club meeting. Then they all shook hands, and Joe Butts went back upstairs.

"We've got a real published author!" Josie hollered, hopping up and down in front of Mariah. "Do you believe it?"

"I think so." Mariah did a couple of hops herself, though she hoped nobody saw her. Hopping didn't seem dignified enough for the President of a successful new club.

6

J oe Butts is my next author of the month," Mariah informed her family at dinner that evening.

"I once heard he lived around here," Mrs. Delany said.

"That's how he happened to see my Benefit Flea Market," Mariah explained, without going into detail.

"Your Benefit Flea what?" Mr. Delany gasped. His eyes darted toward the nearest bookshelf. "What have you been selling, Mariah?"

"Only comics and toys," she assured him. "Mine."

"Your meeting was such a disappointment, I thought you would forget about the club," he said.

"Forget about my club?" It was Mariah's turn to gasp. "This club is the best idea I've ever had. It's got everything. There's a real demand for it."

"A Real Demand?" Mrs. Delany winced. "This sounds like business again. Instead of Lending Libraries and Author-of-the-Month Clubs, why can't you sit down with a good book and enjoy it, Mariah?"

"I can do that, too," Mariah answered, her cheeks full of spaghetti. "But there's more to life."

"You mean wheeling and dealing," her mother said disapprovingly.

"I mean something that makes everything . . ." She tried to come up with the word for what she felt. ". . . fun? interesting? exciting?" But from the expressions on her parents' faces she knew they simply could not understand. She wondered if her friends really did.

As soon as dinner was over, Mariah called Leah to tell her the news.

"That's great!" Leah yelped. "Now I've got something to put on the fliers."

Mariah dialed Emma. "You know you can always count on ME," Emma gushed. "Remember, I contributed the cookies."

Mariah knew she could always count on Emma for one thing: never letting her forget those cookies.

Mrs. Levine called. "The pictures I took aren't developed yet, but as soon as they are I'll get them to you." She spoke in the rapid-fire way that left Mariah wondering what exactly she had said. "Josie tells me you've signed Joe Butts. Good for you. You've got yourself a real author, Mariah."

Yes, a real author would be at her next meeting. Mariah flopped on her bed and hugged her pillow and gazed out the window. That was when she noticed that the little begonia had lost its brown

44

spots. There was a lovely pinkish tinge to the leaves. She wondered why. She had not changed the plant's location, soil, or watering system. She reached for her science folder and wrote, "April 9. Begonia looks good. Leaves are pinkish. Brown spots gone."

"I still don't have a project for you," she told the plant. "But at least I know how to get authors. I need one more for this year and eight for next." She counted on her fingers. "One a month from October through May. I'll set up flea markets in front of houses where they live and write each name on my sign, just like today." Mariah remembered that Joe Butts had said he would have answered if she had written to invite him. "I'll write letters, too," she decided. "All I need are addresses. But where do I get them?" No sooner had she asked herself the question than she knew the answer. The New York Public Library.

"Where have you been?" Lizzy Phipps, the librarian of the upstairs children's room, asked Mariah the following afternoon. "You haven't come in to volunteer for weeks."

Mariah recalled how after her Lending Library disaster she had helped out at the Public Library almost every day. In her time of trouble, the library always made her feel better.

Lizzy Phipps lowered her voice to a whisper. "What's up?"

Mariah told her about the Author-of-the-Month Club.

"What an original idea! Is there anything I can do to help?"

"I need to know where authors live," Mariah said.

Lizzy Phipps went to a shelf near her desk and took out a thick volume: *Something About the Author.* "You won't find addresses, but the names of the publishers are listed," she said. "You can look in the telephone directory for the publishers' addresses and write to your authors in care of them. They'll forward your letters." She handed Mariah the book. "Good luck."

Mariah settled at a table with the volume of authors' names, flipping through the pages, searching for authors who lived in New York City, or those she had heard of. In no time, she had four names. Their bios said they lived in New York City. Suddenly Mariah's eye fell on a name that sent her heart racing. "Obermeyer, T. M. Author of the five Fanny Frost books. Divides her time between a New York City apartment and a farm in New Zealand." Mariah skipped to the end and jotted down the name of the publisher. As she did so, she felt as if Fanny Frost, "round as a pincushion, crusty as a pretzel, and cheerful as a patchwork quilt," were watching her from across the table. Fanny Frost was cook to the Picket family on a sheep station in New Zealand. On first meeting,

Fanny appeared strict and sometimes even harsh. But when you got to know her (as all her lucky readers did), you learned that she was not only funny and mischievous, warm and wise, but possessed of powers that enabled her to take the Picket children on amazing adventures.

"Did you find what you need?" Lizzy Phipps leaned over Mariah's shoulder.

"Mostly," Mariah said. "Only I wish there was an address for T. M. Obermeyer."

Lizzy Phipps laughed. "She gave a talk at the library, and it was my great honor to drive her home. Believe me, Mariah, you don't want her for your guest."

"Where does she live?" Mariah asked.

"That big brownstone building on Central Park West in the Eighties. I think it's called the Daphne."

"The Daphne." Mariah jotted the name in her notebook and underlined it three times.

"You've got a good selection there," Lizzy Phipps said. "Just forget about T. M. Obermeyer."

Forget about T. M. Obermeyer? Mariah thought to herself. Not a chance.

That night after dinner Mariah wrote:

Dear Author,
    Could you come and visit the Mariah Delany Author-of-the-Month Club and tell us

47

about your books and your writing and answer our questions? Each month we ask an author to come and read and share their work with us. We can't offer money because we don't have any. But we promise to read your books and be super thrilled and excited if you would please say yes. If you're interested, here is my number.

Very truly yours,
Mariah Delany

Mariah signed off with her address and phone number. She copied four letters in her best script on the lined lavender stationary Leah had given her for her birthday. The authors were Adams, Bennet, Browder, and Cowper. (She had other plans for T. M. Obermeyer.) In the New York telephone directory Mariah found the addresses of each of their publishers. She carefully addressed the letters and marked them "Please Forward." After she had stamped the envelopes, Mariah went to bed. She wanted to be fresh for the next day, when she would put her T. M. Obermeyer Guest Speaker Plan into action.

Mariah called Josie as soon as she woke up. "Remember you told me that tap dancing was your other talent?"

"Sure," Josie said. "I have three routines."

"Bring your tap shoes and your little dance

floor," Mariah said, "and meet me in the lobby in an hour."

"I don't get it," Josie said.

"You will," Mariah promised.

She turned over the sign and wrote on the back in Magic Marker:

AUTHORS FOR KIDS
A TAP-DANCE BENEFIT TO ENRICH
YOUNG READERS. HELP US PAY LEGENDARY
T. M. OBERMEYER TO APPEAR AS OUR GUEST SPEAKER
AT THE MARIAH DELANY AUTHOR-OF-THE-MONTH CLUB

On the short walk over to Central Park West, Mariah and Josie hardly spoke. "I can't believe I'm going to do this," Josie said.

"You'll be fine," Mariah assured her. "I'll help you count out the beats."

In front of the Daphne they carefully arranged the sign and Josie's little folding wooden dance floor. It was like an exercise mat made of wood. Josie put on her shoes and stood in the middle of the floor. She looked at Mariah, who nodded. Then Josie counted, "One, two, three," and started to dance. Under her breath she began to sing, "When we're out together dancing cheek to cheek." Very soon her face was burning, her eyes glassy. She seemed to be in a world of her own. Her legs moved like a mechanical egg beater; her feet clattered like a windup toy's. It was a chilly morning. A few

people hurried by, glanced at Josie, read the sign, and smiled. Nobody actually laughed, but nobody opened a wallet or a purse either. A uniformed doorman glared. Finally, at the end of her second routine, when Josie's breathing was more like that of a fish out of water, an elderly woman called out, "Good heavens, what a coincidence."

Josie stopped dancing and smiled radiantly. "Do I remind you of Ginger Rogers?"

The woman shook her head. "T. M. Obermeyer

lives in this very building," she said. "But she's not at all the sort of person to visit with children. I hope you know that."

Mariah nodded as if she did, but to herself she thought that the woman obviously had never read the Fanny Frost stories. If she had, she would know that even though Fanny seemed strict and forbidding on the outside, underneath she was warm and wise, and the Picket children adored her.

A group of young mothers and small children emerged from the lobby of the Daphne and drifted toward the sign.

"Start dancing," Mariah urged Josie in a whisper.

Josie took a deep breath and began to dance, but her windup-toy tapping was wearing down. Her red knees looked stiff.

"You know that T. M. Obermeyer lives here?" one of the young mothers said to Mariah.

"I was just telling her that," the elderly woman said. "And that she's not the sort you'd want to have visit."

The young woman nodded. "Unless the event were to be covered by a television station or a newspaper or magazine. Then she can be quite charming. Remember when they came to interview her for that TV show? She loved it."

"We had television lights all over the lobby," the elderly woman recalled. "She was hospitable to the *New York Times* and the *Ladies' Home*

Journal, too. It's just her readers she won't see."

"It's hard to imagine why, what with this being the fiftieth anniversary of the first Fanny Frost book," the younger woman added.

"Stop!" Mariah burst out. "That's it."

Josie's tap shoes clattered to a halt, her knees buckled, and she collapsed on her platform. She was dripping with perspiration.

"No, not you," Mariah told her. "Keep going." Her nose was doing a familiar twitch as she headed for the doorman. "Excuse me. Would you please ring up Ms. Obermeyer?"

"Ms. Obermeyer?" he repeated unbelievingly.

"It's fifteen D," the elderly woman called. "Give it a try, Dennis. She may be home."

Dennis picked up the intercom and pressed a button. Then he handed the receiver to Mariah. There was a click and a bit of static and someone said, "Hello."

"Ms. Obermeyer?" Mariah said.

"Yes?"

Mariah took a deep breath. "I am Mariah Delany from the Mariah Delany Author-of-the-Month Club. We're down here in front of your building running a tap-dance benefit to raise money to help pay for your guest appearance at our club to celebrate the fiftieth anniversary of Fanny Frost with a national magazine that I know will want to . . ."

"Spare yourself," the voice interrupted. "I don't

speak to children's groups." The phone went dead. For a moment Mariah wondered if she had, too. Slowly she handed the receiver back to Dennis.

"I told you it was pointless," the elderly woman said. "If you aren't *Time, Newsweek,* or *Woman's Horizon,* forget it."

"I'm not forgetting it," Mariah said.

"Good luck to you, then." The young woman waved as she walked off. "It's a good idea."

"It's a sensational idea," Mariah corrected her.

"Maybe tap dancing *isn't* my other talent," Josie said, groaning.

Mariah helped her to her feet and they folded up the dance floor. All the while, she was composing the letter she would write as soon as she got home.

"What's the name of that magazine you said your mother works for?" she asked Josie. "And where are they located?"

"*Woman's Horizon,*" Josie said. "On Madison and Fifty-fifth. Do I have to tap-dance for them too?"

"This is the fiftieth anniversary of the first Fanny Frost. T. M. Obermeyer should know that she has a whole new generation of fans. She should meet her readers. She can meet them at my club. A magazine should write about it."

"A magazine?" Josie limped behind Mariah.

"*Woman's Horizon.*" Mariah waited for her to

catch up. "Don't you get it, Josie? *Woman's Horizon* plus T. M. Obermeyer equals our next meeting."

Josie looked too exhausted to get anything, but she stopped and clapped her hands. "That is a real brainstorm, Mariah," she acknowledged wearily.

"Tell your mother," Mariah said.

That night Mariah herself called Mrs. Levine.

"Josie is in bed resting," Mrs. Levine said, "but she told me about your proposal. It sounds interesting. The magazine might go for it."

After this, Mariah sat down and wrote the letter she had been concocting in her mind all afternoon.

> Dear T. M. Obermeyer,
>
> *Woman's Horizon* magazine says they could really go for a story on you being a guest at my club. Since it's the fiftieth anniversary of Fanny Frost, shouldn't everybody know that you have a whole new generation of fans?
>
> Sincerely,
> Mariah Delany, President,
> the Mariah Delany
> Author-of-the-Month Club

Mariah carefully made a copy. She wanted it to look professional. She even looked up how to spell "anniversary." Mrs. Demot would be proud of her, but she knew she couldn't tell Mrs. Demot what she had done. Her teacher would only complain that Mariah had looked up "anniversary" for a letter instead of doing her homework assignments for school.

The next morning she mailed the copy of the letter to T. M. Obermeyer's publisher and hand-delivered the original to T. M. Obermeyer's doorman, Dennis, at the Daphne.

7

For the next two weeks Mariah was in full gear. "Oh, boy, I'm whizzing," she sang in the shower. She had to set up the Joe Butts meeting. She collected file cards left over from the Lending Library, rubber bands and paper clips and rolls of Scotch tape from her father's desk, and took from the wall an unused calendar the bank had put out. She wanted a special club calendar to keep track of club dates. Every afternoon she went through the mail on the foyer table, excitedly searching for letters from the authors she'd written to. What about T. M. Obermeyer? Would she write? Call? Mariah could hardly wait. There was so much to do. Being in business again gave her something to look forward to. She hadn't felt so good since her Lending Library enterprise.

"We have to get the word out," Mariah said to Leah. "We need a full house so Joe Butts knows that we're a serious club."

"I could do fliers on colored paper," Leah said, "and put them on everyone's desk in the morning." She paused and bit her lip. "I'm sorry I wasn't much help till now, Mariah. I guess you really didn't have anybody to count on."

"I had Josie," Mariah reminded her.

"Is she a vice president?" Leah seemed worried.

"That's a good idea." Mariah had never thought of it. "Vice President in Charge of Author Appearances."

Leah's face twitched.

"You could be Vice President in Charge of Promotion," Mariah decided on the spot.

Leah grinned as if she had just received a present. "There will be colored fliers on top of every desk," she assured Mariah.

At lunch Mariah told Dave Peterson, "As Vice President in Charge of Posters, you will need to make one for each homeroom bulletin board and one for the library."

"Don't you need a Vice President in Charge of Disguising the Authors?" Suzy teased. "Someone who can dress writers up in big hats and dark glasses and lots of makeup so no one will know who they are."

Mariah glared. "Joe Butts is our next guest. He is not the Mystery Author" — she paused — "and you're not funny."

"One meeting doesn't make a club," Suzy snapped.

"Just wait till the meeting after Joe Butts." Mariah smiled smugly. "It will blow your socks off."

"T. M. Obermeyer, I suppose." Suzy rolled her eyes.

Later that day, Mrs. Lipson, the school librarian, stopped Mariah on her way to art class. "I notice the posters about your meeting," she said. "There's a great demand for Outlaw Joe books in the library. I don't have enough. Could the author help us?"

As soon as she got home, Mariah checked the mail on the hall table for something from T. M. Obermeyer or *Woman's Horizon*. Nothing yet. Then she called Joe Butts. "Everybody will read your books if they're lucky enough to get hold of one before the meeting. There's a long waiting list," she told him.

"I'll drop off a carton in the mailroom," Joe Butts said. "Your club can buy them at the discount rate I get."

When Mariah hung up the phone, she smiled to herself. She felt like she was running a book club as well as an Author-of-the-Month Club. There were many things to keep track of now. She began to set up her desk. She'd have to get busy.

She cleared away a pile of unfinished math assignments and the history sheet she hadn't gotten to. Behind these she found the nearly empty science folder, "Observing Plant Life." Guiltily, she turned to observe the begonia on the windowsill. It still looked good, even though she hadn't thought up a project yet. She had till the twelfth of May, one whole month. Suddenly she had an idea. What if she sent a plant (the Levines had plenty to spare) to T. M. Obermeyer? She would enclose a note. "Dear T. M. Obermeyer," Mariah began to write on the back of her math assignment sheet. "I hope this plant will remind you that all your fans at the Mariah Delany Author-of-the-Month Club are crossing their fingers and hoping you'll say yes." She copied this note on her lavender stationary, called Josie on the house phone, and told her to select a nice little potted plant to bring with her to school the following day. When this was done, Mariah took the old shoebox and file cards that were left over from her Lending Library. On each card she printed the name of a member and the words "Book Order." She used a red pencil for the members' names and arranged the cards in alphabetical order.

Mrs. Delany knocked on the door. "Oh, Mariah!" she exclaimed happily. "What a lovely sight. You at your desk."

"It's a good place to work," Mariah said. "I didn't even have to buy anything this time. I had everything I needed right here."

"Of course you did, dear. I'm so delighted to see you at work, I nearly forgot to tell you that it's time to set the table for dinner." She hesitated. "But if you're in the middle, I won't interrupt."

"I'm finished for now." Mariah stood up. "I was just making sure that everybody who gets an Outlaw Joe pays for it."

"Is Outlaw Joe a figure in American history?"

"He's a figure in a Joe Butts book."

Mariah and her mother stared at each other.

"You were working on your club and not your history homework," Mrs. Delany said with a heavy sigh of disappointment.

"My next meeting," Mariah said, nodding.

"And maybe your last. Your report from school said you were not doing your homework, Mariah."

"I'll take care of it," Mariah murmured. "I promise."

"Can you promise me that you won't fall behind in your schoolwork because of this club?"

"I promise," Mariah repeated as a small throb

of worry began to pong just inside her forehead. Could she really come through on this promise? Perhaps one day she could appoint a Vice President in Charge of Unfinished Homework.

The very next afternoon Mariah and Leah went to the Daphne with the little plant Josie had brought to school.

"Hello, Dennis," Mariah greeted the doorman.

"Hello, miss." He actually tipped his head at her. "Any luck?"

"Not yet." Mariah handed him the plant and her note. "Could you send these up to T. M. Obermeyer? Maybe they'll help."

"I wouldn't count on it."

"Then put in a good word for me."

To Mariah's surprise, he burst out laughing. "The best words I could put in would be . . . 'Don't do it.' "

Back at Mariah's building a carton full of Joe Butts books was waiting in the mailroom. Leah helped Mariah lug it up to her apartment.

"I'm happy to be working on this club," Leah said.

"I'm happy you are, too," Mariah said, panting. She'd never have been able to carry the box of books by herself. She put the box down and shuffled through the mail on the hall table. Nothing.

Leah held up an Outlaw Joe book and admired

it. "Some people think you'll get Irwin into a disguise and try to pass him off as Joe Butts, the way you tried to pass off Josie Levine. But I tell them even though you talk things up and exaggerate a lot, you wouldn't go that far."

Mariah was suddenly a lot less happy about Leah's working with her on the club than she had been a few minutes before. In fact, she was right in the middle of wishing Leah would go home when the doorbell rang.

It was Josie Levine in dark glasses and long skirt.

"Why are you in your reading clothes?" Mariah asked.

"I have come on Author-of-the-Month Club business," she explained, giving Leah a suspicious glance.

"Leah is Vice President in Charge of Promotion," Mariah said. "You can talk."

Josie sat down and arranged her skirt, crossing her legs and folding her hands on her knee. "Something big is happening," she said slowly. "Something . . . T.M."

Mariah gasped. "She'll do it?"

"Don't know for sure." Josie shook her head. "She called her publisher. Her publisher called the magazine."

"What are you talking about?" Leah demanded.

"I'm afraid I can't tell you at the moment," Mariah said, tipping her head back slightly in a gesture she had once seen the Queen of England

62

use. "I don't want to sound like a person who just talks things up and exaggerates a whole lot."

At eight-thirty that evening Mariah got a phone call from Mrs. Levine. "Obermeyer's publisher called," she said in her rapid-fire way. "To celebrate the fiftieth anniversary of the publication of the first Fanny Frost book, they want to publicize her not only as a legendary author, but as one whose books are popular with today's readers."

Mariah was speechless. This was just what she had suggested!

"The editors at *Woman's Horizon* think that a meeting of your club where Obermeyer is the guest might make a nice short article with photographs."

This had been exactly Mariah's idea, too. Her letter must have done some good.

"We don't know yet if Obermeyer will agree, but we'd like to come to your Joe Butts meeting to see if we really want to go ahead with the idea. I need to speak to your mother or father to get consent."

This had *not* been exactly Mariah's idea. However, she turned the phone over to Mr. Delany, who smiled uneasily. "Yes, I'm aware of the club and of the meetings," he said while Mrs. Delany groaned in the background. "No, I don't feel any harm could come of the magazine's visit. There would be an adult present, the housekeeper. Yes, it is a clever idea." He nodded without enthusiasm.

63

"Yes, Mariah does come up with ingenious plans."
He rolled his eyes toward his wife, who groaned
again.

Mariah heaved a sigh of relief and hurried to her
room. She was so excited she scarcely knew what
to do. Her tattered math workbook lay on the floor
near her desk. She picked it up and flipped through
the pages she was supposed to have finished. There
was a math test coming up soon, but a far more
important test would be the one her club would
take for *Woman's Horizon*. If they passed that one,
there would be an article. What would they write?
Mariah wondered as she gazed at her math sheets.

Woman's Horizon presents
Mariah Delany's Author-of-the-Month
Club

The story of a fifth-grader with a real flair
for organization and a brilliant idea to enrich the lives of her classmates and bring
the great T. M. Obermeyer into her living
room and yours.

There would be photographs. She would wear
her new green pullover which made her look fifteen, and the socks Suzy had given her for her
birthday with hearts up the sides. Maybe after the
magazine article she would be asked to form new
clubs, or travel around the country talking about
how she had put her club together. She might be
interviewed on TV. In fact, maybe there would be

a special! She wished her hair were long enough to go back in a bow. She wished she had pierced ears.

When she next looked at her math workbook, it was nine-fifteen. She wished she had done her math, but it was too late to think straight. The little begonia caught her eye. It looked like a different plant! It was full of buds. "My begonia is about to flower," she quickly wrote in her science folder, and got ready for bed.

8

Before Mariah knew it, Tuesday had turned into Wednesday. There was still no final word about T. M. Obermeyer, but she couldn't worry about that now. If *Woman's Horizon* didn't like the Joe Butts meeting, there wouldn't be any Obermeyer meeting to think about. The only thing on Mariah's mind was her Joe Butts meeting. She even forgot about the homework she had forgotten to do. It wasn't until history class, when Mr. Terril called on her to tell the class about the chapter "Everyday Life in Colonial Times," that she remembered the assignment.

"There weren't any modern things like television and microwave ovens," she guessed. "And telephones and dishwashers and washing machines and dryers and flush toilets and air conditioners and planes and . . ."

Mr. Terril put up his hand to stop her. "Instead of giving us a list of what wasn't, would you please tell us something about what was?"

Mariah looked about her for help.

Suzy's mouth began to move in large, helpful shapes.

Mariah tried to lip-read. "People had to do everything," she mouthed in imitation of Suzy. "Bake their own bread and even make their own brother by beating greens in a churn."

"Suzy seems to be trying to tell you something," Mr. Terril interrupted over the laughter. "Perhaps she could tell you that coming to class unprepared is a poor idea." He paused to give Mariah a chance to sit down. "People made their own butter. They beat cream in a churn, Mariah. I don't want to leave the class with the wrong impression."

After class Mr. Terril told Mariah that if she didn't improve quickly, her final grade would be as poor as her class work. "I know you put a great deal of work into your club. I see the signs for your meeting all over school. But you must remember, Mariah, your first priority is your schoolwork."

"Priority?" Mariah wasn't sure what this meant.

"You have to choose what is most important to put your best effort into."

"My club," Mariah said, answering before she could stop herself.

As if this weren't bad enough, the next class of the day was science. Mrs. Demot went up and down the rows of desks, flipping through the pages in each student's Independent Science Project folder. At Mariah's desk she picked up the one page and frowned. "Where is the rest?"

When Mariah didn't answer, Mrs. Demot turned the page over. "This is it?" She began to read. "April first. The leaves have brownish spots. They droop. My plant looks awful. April ninth. Begonia looks good. Leaves are pinkish. Brown spots gone." She put the page back in Mariah's folder. "What are you doing, Mariah?"

"Observing my plant," Mariah responded miserably.

"But you haven't set up a problem. You have no material. How can you draw a conclusion?"

"I don't know yet," Mariah whispered.

"If this independent project is not completed in a satisfactory way by the twelfth of May, I will have to fail you for the term. 'My plant looks awful' is not a scientific description or conclusion."

Mariah quickly glanced around. She hoped no one had seen or heard Mrs. Demot. She wished she hadn't.

As soon as the last bell rang, Mariah grabbed her jacket from her locker and ran all the way home. She had other things to think about.

The first meeting of her club had been a good dress rehearsal. This time, setting up for the meeting was a breeze. Mariah and Mrs. Todd arranged chairs without any uncertainty as to where they should go. There was no last-minute fiddling with trays. Mariah knew exactly which ones would work best. She set up her chair in the foyer along with the little folding table. On the table she stacked unsold copies of the Outlaw Joe books.

This time when the doorbell began to ring, Mariah went to open it, full of confidence and anticipation. In only ten minutes every seat in the room was filled. Six people said they didn't mind sitting on the floor. Mrs. Levine and a man in a dark suit named Andrew from *Woman's Horizon* said they preferred to stand at the back. Just as she was beginning to wonder when Joe Butts would arrive, the bell rang again. Mariah grabbed the knob and flung the door open. A tall masked stranger leaned into the Delany foyer. His hands were on his hips, where a holster hung low. "Howdee, ma'am." In the holster Mariah saw a gun.

She was speechless with terror. Her mother had always warned her to call out "Who is it?" before opening the door. With all the excitement of the meeting, she had forgotten.

"Hey now, little lady." The man began to laugh. "Don't take on. It's me, Outlaw Joe." He took off the mask.

"Joe Butts." Mariah nearly fell down with relief.

"This must be a good disguise," Joe Butts said, replacing the mask. "Now, where's my audience?" He strode before Mariah right into the living room.

"'Scuse me." Joe Butts tipped his cowboy hat at

the club members in a menacing way. "Joe Butts was sick this mornin', and he asked me could I take his place. I'm Outlaw Joe."

Mariah watched as the look of confusion on her club members' faces turned to dread. A few people glanced toward the door as if they wanted to make a run for it. How could she reassure them and let them know that this was a joke? What about Mrs. Levine and Andrew? Mrs. Levine caught Mariah's eye and winked, as if to say, "Don't worry. I'll take care of this."

"You can't fool me, Outlaw Joe," Mrs. Levine called out gaily. "Joe Butts isn't sick. He's hiding behind that mask."

Mariah wanted to kiss Mrs. Levine on the spot, even if she might decide not to do an article on the club.

Joe Butts pulled the mask off his face and grinned. "You may just be right, ma'am," he said. "Sick or well or in hiding, Outlaw Joe is a real good guy with a heart of gold. It's living in the old West made him seem hard and mean. In the Montana Territory back before it was a state, if you didn't know how to take care of yourself somebody'd sure do it for you and you'd be a sorry man. Back then in Virginia City, with the gold prospectors and the covered wagons coming through and some of the sheriffs and their agents turning mean and corrupt, the outlaws were sometimes the ones who had to keep the law and order. Outlaws like me, Outlaw Joe."

Even though the audience seemed to relax, Mariah couldn't help wishing her first *real* author hadn't come in disguise like her first fake author. Outlaw Joe demonstrated how to make a quick draw and the different ways of wearing a cowboy hat, and finally he "allowed as how when I'm deep in one of my stories, if you tapped me on the shoulder, I'd as like answer to the name Outlaw Joe Brady as I would to Writer Joe Butts."

Everybody laughed with relief.

When he finished his talk, there was a question from every club member.

"Where do you get your ideas?"

"Do you make up your own titles?"

"Do you make up the names of characters?"

"How did you become a writer?"

"What's your favorite book?"

The hands kept waving and Joe Butts kept answering until a faint pinging sound from his alarm watch reminded him that it was five o'clock and time to get back to work on the seventh book about Outlaw Joe.

Everybody gave him a big hand and shouted, "Thank you!"

Outlaw Joe put his mask over his face, tipped his hat, and waved "So long." But club members crowded around him for his autograph in their copies of his books. Members who hadn't bought books asked to buy them. Some people still owed money for the books they had purchased. With the shoebox of membership cards before her and her sharp pencil poised for action, Mariah began to sign up members, sell new books, and collect money for old ones. It was finally happening. She was in business again.

Mrs. Levine and the man from *Woman's Horizon* took snapshots of her making change, adding to her list, trying to keep membership cards in order.

"I'll sign up members while you collect for

books," Suzy volunteered. "Gosh, it's taking off, Mariah."

"What about me?" Emma reached for the membership box. "I want to be part of this thing, you know. And I'm better at writing small than Suzy is. Don't forget, I supported this club right from the beginning. I did cookies when nobody believed in you, Mariah."

Mariah handed the shoebox and pencil to Suzy. "Emma can call out the names while you write them down," she said diplomatically.

"Does this make Suzy some sort of vice president?" Emma asked.

"Vice President in Charge of Membership," Mariah said distractedly. She was busy making change.

"Since I did cookies when nobody else believed in you, I think I should be a Vice President in Charge of something," Emma said, pouting.

"I'll think of something," Mariah assured her. But all she could think was how amazing it was that her friends who had thought the Author-of-the-Month Club was an impossible idea were now competing to be made vice presidents!

She handed Joe Butts the money she had collected for his books. Every one of them had been sold. He thanked Mariah for inviting him, put the envelope in his pocket, waved good-bye, and got on the elevator as Mrs. Delany stepped off.

"Is this my floor?" Mrs. Delany seemed confused by all the people in the hallway.

"I've had a real success!" Mariah shouted when she saw her mother making her way toward their apartment door.

"Oh, dear," Mrs. Delany murmured.

"Mariah's done a remarkable job," Mrs. Levine told Mrs. Delany. "You should be proud."

Mrs. Delany put down her briefcase and gazed at the chairs every which way in the living room and the juice cups and cookie crumbs. "I just hope she cleans up."

"That's it, Emma!" Mariah called. "You are Vice President in Charge of Cleaning Up."

"That doesn't sound very vice presidential," Emma said uncertainly, not knowing whether to be pleased or not. But she did begin to stack the folding chairs.

"Vice President in Charge of Cleaning Up?" Mrs. Delany turned to Mariah and smiled incredulously. "You really have had a success," she said.

9

The living room was packed," Mrs. Delany told Mr. Delany and Irwin that night at dinner. "And there sat our Mariah, cool as a cucumber, appointing a Vice President in Charge of Cleaning Up."

"Mariah the Club President," her father quipped.

Irwin grinned at her across the table. "Congratulations, Maisie," he said.

Mariah tipped her head, graciously accepting their praise. Pride filled her like a delicious, long-awaited treat, better than any chocolate. At last she had done something right. At last they appreciated her. She even looked forward to school the next day. Would her classmates add their congratulations to her parents' and brother's?

But when Mariah arrived in Mrs. Demot's room the following morning, everyone seemed distracted and nervous. Why didn't they compliment her on yesterday's meeting? Just as she was asking herself this question, Mariah saw Mrs. Demot passing out paper. A math quiz! Her question was answered.

Unfortunately, it was the only question answered. The test turned out to cover pages she had scarcely had time to look at, much less learn. When she handed in her paper, Mariah knew it represented a new low in her growing list of poor scores. She tried to cheer herself by thinking about the Author-of-the-Month Club and imagining what would happen if T. M. Obermeyer agreed to be her next guest.

However, nothing could have prepared Mariah for the telephone call she received that very afternoon when she got home from school.

"Mrs. Levine for Mariah Delany," a secretary said.

"Mariah!" It was Mrs. Levine. "It's fantastic! T. M. Obermeyer has agreed."

T. M. Obermeyer in her very own living room? Mariah stopped listening to Mrs. Levine. She couldn't believe it! She was thinking how one thing led to another. All her planning, her flea markets, benefits, letters, had led to some phone calls and now this . . . a miracle.

"We'll go over the details later," Mrs. Levine was saying. "I'll have to know how many will be coming. We'll have our staff photographers, my assistant, and the publicity person from the publisher. The magazine will provide refreshments this time and the chairs. Let me tell you the dates that work for T.M.," and she rattled off several dates in May. Mariah picked the soonest. She couldn't wait.

"Then let's make that firm," Mrs. Levine said. "May third. First Wednesday. T. M. Obermeyer. I leave it to you to spread the word at school. The club should be exactly as we saw it at your meeting. That was the right number, no more, no less. It has to look natural, and we don't want T.M. to be annoyed by a crowd of noisy children. I'll keep you posted on any developments." Her voice was fading. She was hanging up.

It took Mariah a few minutes to realize that the conversation had ended. She sat gazing dazedly at the telephone before replacing the receiver. She even wondered if the conversation had happened. Had she dreamed it?

What would her friends say? Her teachers? Her parents? There was no one at home to tell. She realized with a pang that her mother and father were going from work to a dinner party. She would be asleep before they got back, and breakfast was such a hurried time no one would pay any attention. Only a few hours before, she had been worried about a silly math test. Now here she was, planning a meeting that would be featured in a national magazine. She looked out the window past the rooftop of a new high-rise building, toward the skyscrapers of downtown. One day everyone working in those buildings would read about her club.

Suddenly she noticed the begonia. It was blooming! Little white flowers hung like delicate wax bells from its slender branches. This was a real good-luck sign, Mariah decided, but it reminded her of the science project she hadn't even started yet. She opened her science folder to enter her observations. As she did so, she wondered why she was bothering. Maybe she should skip school altogether and work on her club full time. She'd bring enrichment to everyone. Perhaps she ought to set up clubs all over the country. All over the world. She'd better get started.

She picked up the telephone. "Emma," she said, "I'm calling a vice presidents' lunch meeting tomorrow. Be there."

10

T. M. Obermeyer," Dave whispered, after Mariah made her announcement at the vice presidents' lunch meeting. "I thought he was dead."

"I hope not," Mariah said, "or she won't be much fun."

"She?" Dave was as surprised to hear that T.M. was a woman as he was to hear she was alive and their next guest.

"Fanny Frost is world famous," Suzy said. "My father read those books in French when he was a boy. There was a Fanny Frost movie before we were even born."

"I can't believe this." Emma summed up the feelings of all of them.

"We need fliers and posters by Monday." Mariah forged ahead. "I know you'll all do your best." To encourage them, she passed around a box of something called Six Feet of Bubble Gum. The gum was rolled in a continuous tape. The vice presidents helped themselves to a couple of inches apiece.

Suzy Bellamy blew a bubble the size of the Goodyear blimp, which burst all over her nose.

"This is what my mom calls a Power Lunch," she said.

Mariah wasn't sure if this was a Power Lunch, but she knew she felt very powerful. As they all stood up to leave, she could tell that this feeling of power was catching. She had passed it along to Emma and Leah and Suzy and Dave and even to Josie.

After lunch Mrs. Demot handed back the math quiz from the day before. "I never got a zero before," Mariah protested weakly.

"You never got every single answer wrong before either," Mrs. Demot pointed out.

"I got my name right," Mariah said.

"That wasn't one of the questions." Mrs. Demot put her arm around Mariah's shoulder. "You've been a million miles away for the last month. It isn't just science and math. Mr. Terril has spoken with me and so have your other teachers. Except for art, where you made a poster for your club, you've been doing practically no schoolwork. You must remember, Mariah, school is the most important thing in your life."

"My club is very important, too," Mariah said.

"Clubs come and go. School is going to be with you for many years."

For a moment Mariah felt like the pendulum on an old clock. *Bong*, she was powerful, important, and practically famous. *Bong*, she was unprepared, nearly failing, and about to be in big trouble with her parents. Swinging back and forth between these two extremes made her feel a little nauseated. "I'll try harder." She sighed.

"That's what you always say." Mrs. Demot sighed back. "And I always want to believe you mean it."

Mariah always did mean it . . . more or less. But suddenly the pendulum swung again, and *bong*, why did she need science and math and history if she could be a success without them? There were just so many other things she needed to do before she did her math. For one thing, she had to write a good introduction speech for T. M. Obermeyer's visit. To do this she'd need to reread the Fanny Frost books, and to reread Fanny Frost, she needed to go to the school library as soon as possible.

Mrs. Lipson, the librarian, greeted Mariah with wide eyes. "Is it true that T. M. Obermeyer will be your next guest author, Mariah?"

"True."

"I can't believe . . . I mean, Mariah, may I join your club? Or at least may I come to that meeting?"

Mariah shook her head. "The magazine wants my club to be exactly the way it was at my last meeting."

"I guess I'll just have to hear about it, then," Mrs. Lipson said good-humoredly, but Mariah had

81

a feeling she was offended. Mrs. Lipson had always been her friend. Mariah felt bad about turning her down.

Mariah settled at a library table with one of the Fanny Frost books, hoping that it would take her mind off feeling bad about Mrs. Lipson. Sure enough, as she began the first words of the first chapter, a curious magic engulfed her. Fanny Frost, "round as a pincushion, crusty as a pretzel, and cheerful as a patchwork quilt," could open an ordinary-looking door and lead one into the most extraordinary adventures. As she read, Mariah wondered if T. M. Obermeyer would look just like Fanny Frost. The idea of Fanny Frost stepping out of a book into real life and her very own living room in the form of T. M. Obermeyer made Mariah dizzy with excitement. She could see plump, cozy Fanny swirling before her in her white apron and long red shawl, standing in her foyer, peeking into the dining room. It was too much. She closed the book at the point when she envisioned Fanny looking into her bedroom. "Sloppy child," Fanny would say.

Mariah took out her calendar and began to count the days till the meeting. Only two weeks. She started to write her introduction.

"Today, I am happy to introduce you to the one and only Fanny Fro" —

Mariah crossed out "Fanny Fro" and wrote "T. M. Obermeyer." Then she crossed out "today."

Then she crossed out the whole line and put her pen away. Maybe her mother could help.

"T. M. Obermeyer here?" Mrs. Delany began to choke.

Irwin and Mr. Delany rose from their seats with concern as she gasped for breath and gulped water.

"Gertrude, what is it?" Mr. Delany asked.

She shook her head helplessly and then said in a thin voice, "Lying on my mat during rest period at Mrs. Schram's School listening to Mrs. Pankhurst read to us from Fanny Frost. I remember it as if it were yesterday. That's when I fell in love with books. I could no more say hello to T. M.

Obermeyer than to the President of the United States. I'd fall down in a dead faint."

"You don't have to be here," Mariah assured her mother. That was all she needed.

"Who is T. M. Obermeyer?" Irwin asked over his soup.

Irwin hardly ever read fiction. Even in the first grade he had begun to immerse himself in the encyclopedia. For once it occurred to Mariah that this habit could be a real asset.

"She's a living legend," Mariah said. "Could you help write an introduction for her?"

Irwin took out a pen and, between spoonfuls of soup, began to scribble on his paper napkin. "A living legend," he repeated as he wrote. "A living legend in the living room. Hey, that's nice. When a living legend turns up in my living room," Irwin wrote, "it's a . . ."

"Shock," Mariah said.

"Miracle," Irwin wrote. "T. M. Obermober."

"T. M. Obermeyer," Mariah corrected him.

"T.M.O. makes miracles happen in real life just the way she does in books." Irwin jotted quickly and looked up in triumph.

"Hooray!" Mariah said. "Irwin, I love you."

"See how books bring us together." Mrs. Delany applauded, smiling at her husband.

The very next day Mariah found samples of posters and fliers on her homeroom desk.

"Mariah Delany," Mrs. Demot called. "Are you reviewing homework?"

"In a way." Mariah tried to slip the papers under her workbook, but not before Mrs. Demot had taken two giant steps to her desk.

"That club again. Mariah, you are not to do club business in school." She snatched up the fliers. "I'll keep these till the end of the day." Mrs. Demot turned to address the class. "What I just told Mariah goes for all of you. Clubs are an after-school activity."

"Then how will I spread the word that my next guest is T. M. Obermeyer?" Mariah asked.

"T. M. Obermeyer?" Mrs. Demot looked at the flier in her hand. "Mariah, is this some sort of let's-pretend?"

Mariah shook her head. "T. M. Obermeyer is coming to speak to my club," she said slowly and distinctly.

"If T. M. Obermeyer is really coming to speak to your club" — Mrs. Demot studied Mariah with her most searching and questioning look — "you don't need any publicity at all. Believe me."

Mrs. Demot was right.

Without a single poster or flier, everybody in the school seemed to have heard who Mariah's next guest would be.

"Would it be okay if I bring a few of the third-graders to your meeting?" Ms. Ramey, the third-

85

grade teacher, ran up to Mariah in the hallway outside the gym. "They love listening to Fanny Frost and I know they'd be good. I'd stay in the background, since it's a club for kids. Obermeyer is my absolute favorite children's author."

"No," Mariah said miserably. It made her feel strange, turning down a librarian and now a teacher. "The magazine says I have to keep the club exactly the way it was at my last meeting."

After school Ms. Ensolm, the assistant principal, was waiting for her bus on the corner when she saw Mariah. "Mariah Delany," she said. "Just the person I want to see."

This was it, Mariah thought. The terrible math scores, the unfinished history assignment, the science project she still hadn't worked out, had all been reported to the principal's office. She was in big trouble.

"Are you inviting any school personnel to your Obermeyer meeting?" Ms. Ensolm asked with a charming smile.

"I can't." Mariah groaned. An odd combination of awkwardness and relief swept over her.

"Who'd know if I stood at the back of the room and listened?"

"The magazine said the meeting had to be exactly the same as the last one," Mariah said hurriedly when she saw the light change, and she ran across the street.

"I could provide my special punch," Ms. Ensolm called after her.

Mariah pretended not to hear. As she jogged home, she counted it up. She had told six teachers, thirty-two third-graders, eight sixth-graders, one librarian, and an assistant principal NO.

How could it be that Ms. Ensolm was asking *her* for a favor? She was the assistant principal. It was as if Mariah's world had tipped and all the people in it had shifted into other places so that she couldn't tell who was who or what to expect of them.

Success was more complicated than she had thought.

11

"Why can't I give out these fliers?" Leah asked dejectedly. "I really worked hard on them."

"Too many people want to come to the meeting as it is," Mariah explained. "We don't need to advertise."

"I gave this poster everything I had." Dave held up the red-and-white masterpiece. "Teague wouldn't let me use school paint. I had to buy my own."

"I'll reimburse you from the club treasury," Mariah said, thinking that soon she would ask for club dues of twenty-five cents per person per meeting. "Maybe we can change the author's name and use it for our next guest."

"There's nothing to do for this meeting," Suzy grumbled.

"I have something to do." Emma grinned. "I have to meet my mother after school to shop for a new dress. She wants me to look my best in *Woman's Horizon*."

"A new dress?" Suzy yelped. "I better get one, too."

Leah's eyes grew very round. "If some Hollywood agent saw how beautiful a person looked in a photograph, it could be the beginning of a career, couldn't it?"

"What career?" Josie asked.

"A modeling career," Leah said. "I need a haircut, too."

"Will the magazine mention us vice presidents by name?" Dave asked.

"I don't know," Mariah murmured, putting her head down on the lunch table. This was something new. Now her vice presidents expected to become famous. The bell rang, and for once, even though she was unprepared for history, Mariah was relieved that lunch was over.

When she got home, Mariah went straight to her closet. She wanted to look like the president and founder of an important club. One glance told her that her wardrobe was all wrong. She checked out her mother's drawers and closet. Sure enough. Mariah pulled a silky black chemise-style dress over her head and, like magic, she was twenty-five. The telephone rang.

Mariah picked up her mother's bedside phone. She pretended she was Mrs. Levine in her office.

"This is long distance. I have a collect call for Ms. Mariah Delany from Mr. Don Cowper in Rapid City. Will you accept the charges?"

"Yes, I am Mariah Delany," Mariah answered excitedly. Don Cowper was one of the authors she had written to! Another letter was about to pay off. In the full-length mirror on her mother's closet door, she watched herself sit down on her parents' bed. She crossed her legs and accepted her first collect call.

"Ms. Delany," a man's voice said, seeming to come from over mountains and plains, "I got your wonderful letter of invitation. I haven't lived in New York City for a couple of years, but my publisher forwarded it to me."

"Oh, great," Mariah said.

"As you know, I write science fiction for ages eight through twelve, and I would like to be your author of the month whenever it's convenient. The middle of May would be best for me."

"The middle of May sounds good," Mariah said. "I'm already booked for the third." She lowered her voice so that it sounded like Mrs. Levine's. "T. M. Obermeyer is in that slot, but I don't see why I couldn't wrap up my first season with two meetings. How about" — she began to flip the pages of her mother's bedside calendar — "the seventeenth?"

"Sounds perfect," Don Cowper said. "Since Obermeyer leaves on the third, it will give me plenty of time to settle in before I address your club."

"Then let's make that firm," Mariah said, trying to sound professional. She wrote the date on her mother's pad. "It's a Wednesday. Four o'clock."

"By the way, I do magic tricks as well as talk about my books." He laughed. "After all, it's important to put on a good show, or you could end up losing your audience. You'll get your money's worth, Ms. Delany."

"You know we can't pay," Mariah said hastily.

"Yup. Don't worry. I'll make things easy for you. My accommodations are my bedroll, and you can reimburse me for the bus. That plus being back in the Big Apple with a room full of my readers is payment enough, if you know what I mean."

Mariah didn't know exactly what he meant, but she laughed, too. He sounded like a funny man. Rapid City sounded like New Jersey. What with

91

talk of reimbursements and long-distance calls from authors, her club seemed to be gaining national popularity. It was like a dream.

"Then it's the seventeenth of May at four o'clock," Mariah said in the Levine Professional Voice.

"But I'll see you before that." He chuckled. "After all, I'm not just your author of the day or the hour, but of the month!"

"Not of the day or the hour, but of the month," Mariah repeated. That could be a good club motto. She gave him her address and he gave her his. Rapid City, South Dakota? Mariah could hardly believe it. News of her club had spread far beyond New York. She told him she was delighted that they were "firm."

After she hung up, she took off her mother's dress and put it away. There was no doubt about it: she needed new clothes. She would ask her mother to take her shopping. She was a successful, soon-to-be-famous person; she couldn't look like a four-year-old or wear other people's clothes.

"I shouldn't have to wear other people's clothes to my meeting," Mariah told her mother as soon as she came home from work.

"I certainly agree with that," Mrs. Delany said. "Since it's exam time right now and I've got a ton of work, I can't take you shopping, but I can pick up something nice for you on my lunch break."

The "something nice" was pale green (to go with her eyes). Mariah thought it made her look at least fourteen, especially if she belted it.

On the morning of May 3, Mariah walked gingerly into the kitchen, hoping she would be able to eat.

"Today's the day, isn't it?" Mrs. Delany greeted her at the breakfast table. "I'm sorry I can't be here to help, but Dr. Milgrim insisted I teach a special afternoon class that will run for two hours."

For once Mariah was grateful to her mother's boss, Dr. Milgrim, who, whenever she saw Mariah, was critical of her for having schemes and enterprises instead of good grades. She didn't want her mother's "dead faint" to be one of the events greeting T. M. Obermeyer. "Everything is all set," she said. "Don't worry."

"I don't." Mrs. Delany smiled. "Especially since you promised me you wouldn't neglect your schoolwork."

That did it for eating breakfast. "I have to get dressed now." Mariah put her uneaten toast and glass of milk in the refrigerator with a silent prayer that she would get through the day.

12

The prayer was not enough. Mrs. Demot called on her twice, even though she must have known after the first time that Mariah was unprepared.

Suzy tried to signal answers, but all Mariah could tell was that Suzy was wearing a new dress in bright red, and so were Leah and Emma. Next to their red dresses her pale green would fade into the wall. Emma had a dazzling hairband with polka dots.

As soon as she got home, Mariah rushed into her mother's bedroom to put on the black chemise. At least it would stand out in a photograph. But it was too long. In fact, it came down to her ankles. It didn't look glamorous, as it had the other day; it looked like a bathrobe! How could she have thought it would work? She pulled it off and tried on a dark purple turtleneck sweater. It looked good on her mother, but it didn't look very good on Mariah. Maybe her mother's new red-flowered ruffled jumper over it would help. It didn't. She tried a jacket over the turtleneck and velvet trousers under the jumper. Finally she took them all off and tried a silk pullover with a flannel skirt and a scarf covered with roses. The doorbell rang before she could decide about it, so she quickly yanked on her blue jeans and favorite old shirt.

Mrs. Levine stood in the foyer with two men from the magazine. They carried photographic lights and a camera. Without saying a word, the three arrivals shot past her to the living room, where they began to work frantically, setting up and positioning the lights. Soon another woman arrived. She was from T. M. Obermeyer's publisher. Her name was Ricky. The men were Andrew, who had been at the Joe Butts meeting, and Ned. In a matter of moments they had pulled the living room sofa over to the window and put the coffee table in the bedroom. Mrs. Levine set a box of Danish pastries on the dining room table with fancy paper plates and flowered paper napkins.

"Should I set up the chairs?" Mariah asked. No one bothered to answer. Then she saw that stacks of chairs were being delivered, lined up like guests in the outer lobby. Mrs. Todd stood in the doorway watching Ricky and Ned unfold the metal chairs and put them in a semicircle around the sofa. Mrs. Levine was arranging the Danish pastry on a platter.

"She's never on time," Ricky told Ned under her breath.

"That could be a real advantage."

95

They both laughed. Mariah stood very still and pretended she wasn't listening.

"I'm really worried about this appearance," Ricky went on.

"But she likes publicity, I hear," Ned said.

"She loves publicity, not her public."

"So you talked her into doing this?"

"That remains to be seen." Ricky looked nervously at her watch.

Mariah felt as if a cube of ice had been deposited in her bloodstream. Her hands were so cold she hugged them under her arms. She could hardly move. In contrast, Mrs. Todd flitted from the kitchen to the living room, watching everything as if it were about to be stolen.

Soon the doorbell began to ring and the club members to arrive. Everybody was dressed up. Helena Murty even had on makeup. Eric Berson was wearing a suit and tie. They looked more as if they were arriving for a birthday party than just a club meeting, and they perched stiffly on the rented chairs, careful not to rumple new clothes.

"Hi, kids." Ricky waved at them like a TV host. "Loosen up a little. Relax. It's only T. M. Obermeyer."

The name made everyone jump a little, as if an electric current had gone through the room.

There was a small commotion near the front door. Mrs. Levine was greeting someone, and then Ricky practically flew to her side.

"She's here," Ned hissed at Andrew. "T.M. Get her entering the room." The camera began to whir and buzz and click.

At first Mariah thought there had to be some mistake. She did not see Fanny Frost "plump as a pincushion, crusty as a pretzel, cheerful as a patchwork quilt." She saw a thin, gray-haired, disgruntled-looking elderly woman in a dark suit, who, if anything, resembled not the cushion but the pin.

"This way, T.M." Ricky guided her by the arm into the living room toward the sofa. "Where do you want her?" she called to Andrew, as if T. M. Obermeyer were a piece of furniture.

"Smack in the middle." He pointed to the center cushion. "Get some of the kids on the floor up close." He was squinting into his viewfinder. "Take away that lamp so they can look up at her."

Quickly, four club members were settled cross-legged on the rug, gazing uncomfortably past T. M. Obermeyer's bony knees into her glinty glasses.

"Looks good," Andrew said.

"Mariah" — Mrs. Levine motioned to her — "begin your meeting."

Mariah took a quick glance at her guest speaker, stood up awkwardly beside the sofa, and delivered Irwin's words of welcome from an index card that shook so violently it seemed to have a life of its own. When she was done, everyone clapped in a mechanical way.

T. M. Obermeyer coughed. "I don't as a rule give talks to my readers," she said in a thin voice. "I would prefer questions." She looked out at them with an expression that was hardly expectant.

A few hands went right up. Some people were as busy looking over their shoulders at the camera as they were trying to get T. M. Obermeyer's attention.

"You." T. M. Obermeyer pointed a finger at Herbie Lustig.

"I was just wondering" — Herbie scratched his ear — "uh, where do you get your ideas from?"

There was a long pause during which T. M. Obermeyer scrunched up her mouth as if she had a bad taste in it. "I have been asked that question at least five hundred times," she complained. "To be honest, I don't for the life of me know. It is really a stupid question. Let's have another." She looked at her audience and raised her brows. No one stirred. Not a soul. Herbie Lustig's face was whitish and weird. T. M. Obermeyer turned and glared at Ricky. "I told you this was pointless. It is a waste of time talking to children. They have no idea at all of what to ask or even think." She waved her hand dismissively to include the entire room. "Basically, what they want is to be entertained. They want someone who will tell them funny stories or do a magic trick. I am not an entertainer. I write books. If my books turn out to be for them" — she looked straight at Mariah — "that's all to the good. If not, that's fine, too."

Frantically, Mariah's eyes circled the room. She had developed a sharp pain at the side of her ribs. Herbie Lustig had developed a rash all over his face and neck. The entire club had developed a look of stunned horror. She had to do something.

"Excuse me," Mariah began.

"Yes." T. M. Obermeyer turned a cold stare on her. "Mariah Delany," she said accusingly. "The one who figured out the clever scheme that would rope me into this. Tap-dancing show in front of my building, the plant with the note, and those letters you sent must have earned you points with your parents and teachers. Maybe *they* fell for it, but I didn't."

Mariah felt as if something very hot had scorched her right through the skin to a place inside herself. "I did not make points with my teachers or parents," she burst out. "They were all against my club, because I worked so hard to get you to come I never did my schoolwork. I'm in trouble with my teachers and my parents!"

"I wish I could say I was sorry," T. M. Obermeyer said. "But, really, who asked you?"

"Nobody!" Mariah cried. It was true. Nobody had asked her!

T. M. Obermeyer began to stand up. "Some of my readers make the mistake of thinking that

99

because I wrote Fanny Frost I am like her. I AM NOT. I made her up because I enjoy writing about amusing, entertaining people who are the opposite of myself. My books are my books. If you like them, read them. If not, don't."

"We read your books," Mariah responded in a choking voice. "We loved them. We are your readers, and if you don't like it, you — you can lump it! I'm sorry I ever asked you to come talk to my club."

For the first time, T. M. Obermeyer smiled. It was a slow smile, but when it arrived, it was as broad and glinty as any of Fanny Frost's. "You really have learned something then," she said. "Just because a book is entertaining, it doesn't mean the author will be. Just because you want the book in your house, it doesn't mean you'll want the author as well."

What Mariah had learned was that she never wished to go through another experience like this as long as she lived.

13

T. M. Obermeyer was gone. So were Andrew and Ned and Ricky and Mrs. Levine and the chair-rental people with the rented chairs and the members of the Author-of-the-Month Club and Mrs. Todd. Only Mariah and a few vice presidents were left. They sat around the dining room table gazing at the platter of leftover Danish pastry. Except for these pastries, the apartment was as it had been before. You never would have known there'd been a meeting. How Mariah wished there hadn't been.

"Why didn't anybody warn us what she'd be like?" Emma asked.

"They did," Mariah confessed. "I just didn't pay attention."

"Don't feel bad." Suzy spoke up suddenly. "It was so awful, it was great. She *is* a little like Fanny Frost. Only when Fanny is 'too honest' in the books, it's fun."

"That's true," Leah chimed in. "I really loved that."

"I loved the way you talked back to her, Mariah," Dave added.

"I didn't love it." Mariah shook her head, but she did love Dave's compliment.

"I hope nothing like this ever happens again," Josie said.

"It won't." Mariah pounded the table decisively. "This club is over."

"How can you say that?" Emma protested. "Just when you've finally got everybody signed up!"

Mariah picked up the copy of a Fanny Frost book that Ricky had left behind. "Books are great." She held it to her chest. "You open them and close them when you want to. They are between two covers. But authors? You never know what to expect!"

"Don't you expect Don Cowper for May seventeenth?" Dave asked.

"Oh, no! I better stop him!" Mariah gasped. The thought of going through another meeting made her feel sick to her stomach.

Suzy eyed the platter of Danish. "Am I the only person who can be upset and hungry at the same time?"

Emma reached for an almond twist. "Everybody left in such a hurry, we forgot to pass them around."

"Isn't that a shame." Suzy grinned, helping herself to a raspberry puff. "I don't like clubs and I'm no joiner, but this was the best club I ever belonged to." She took a bite. "That has nothing to do with the refreshments, either."

Knowing Suzy, Mariah doubted this, but she thanked her anyway.

After they left, Mariah went to her room. Only a short time ago, that very morning, she had left it, feeling full of anticipation and excitement. Now she looked around her. The room she always loved as her safe place, her sanctuary, gave her no comfort. It seemed to reflect her mood of failure and hurt and betrayal. The curtains on either side of her window looked gray and stained. The begonia on the sill, which just that morning had been blooming, was losing its flowers. They stuck to the ledge like old snow. Some of them had fallen on the rug, where they drifted in brownish heaps. The leaves of the plant were dull and drooping. Feeling the way the begonia looked, Mariah went to her desk and opened her science folder. She still had no idea for a project. She hadn't thought up a problem. She hadn't done any schoolwork for days. Her meeting was a disaster. Her club was finished. She needed to get in touch with Don Cowper right away and tell him not to come. She was glad she'd thought to write down his address and phone number. Just as she was about to go to the phone, she heard her mother's key in the lock and her customary call, "I'm home, everyone," followed by an uncustomary "Mariah, come tell us about your meeting."

Us? . . . Who was "us"?

"In a minute," Mariah called back. She went to

the bathroom and washed her hot face and combed her hair. Her reflection in the mirror reminded her of the begonia. Dull and drooping.

"Mariah," Mrs. Delany called through the bathroom door and then opened it a crack. "Dr. Milgrim is here. She asked me to recommend a restaurant in our neighborhood so that she could make her eight o'clock meeting at the university, and I had to invite her to dinner." Mrs. Delany whispered all this in the nervous voice that her boss, Dr. Milgrim, always evoked in her. "She's as eager to hear about this afternoon as I am. Do me a favor. Please come in and talk to her while I fix dinner."

If Mariah had been asked how this afternoon could be even worse than it already was, she couldn't have come up with anything. But without meaning to, her mother had. Dr. Milgrim.

Mariah stalled for time. She combed her hair and then she brushed it. She could just hear Dr. Milgrim gloating over her club's failure. "You see, Gertrude, it's what I always tell you. Children today have no discipline. They don't know how to work. We give them too much leeway. Clubs, ha! Ridiculous! They should concentrate on the basics. They should be getting an education, and I don't mean after-school fun and games." What should she say about her meeting? First she decided to lie, then she decided to tell the truth, and finally she decided to avoid the subject completely. She went into the living room.

Dr. Milgrim was settled on the sofa in the exact spot where T. M. Obermeyer had ruined Mariah's club. With a glass of sherry in her hand, she munched celery sticks from a tray full of olives and cut vegetables set before her on the coffee table. "Mariah Delany," she boomed. "I hear you have a thrilling event to report to us."

At this moment, Mr. Delany opened the front door. Irwin was just behind him. "Ah, Dr. Milgrim," he greeted her, with surprise that luckily sounded like pleasure. Irwin grimaced slightly. Mariah knew this was not only because he disliked Dr. Milgrim as much as she did, but because he knew there would be a little less for dinner and that whatever it was would be burned or underdone because Dr. Milgrim made his mother so nervous.

"I was just asking Mariah to tell about her club meeting," Dr. Milgrim said.

"She mustn't say a word until we can all hear." Mr. Delany winked at Mariah and went to hang up his coat.

Just then Mrs. Delany returned to the room with bowls of peanuts and crackers.

"It's my turn to set the table," Mariah said and quickly made her escape. She arranged the good dishes and fancier paper napkins as slowly as possible, while her poor, frantic mother went about scorching the rice and splattering blender soup all over the countertop. Even so, before long Mrs. Delany was calling them in for dinner.

Irwin lumbered into the dining room and pulled out his chair. It gave Mariah a small, guilty pang of relief to think that it was his turn to clean up tonight.

"This is called Hasty Soup," Mrs. Delany said, describing the thick vichyssoise she'd made by dumping a can of cream of potato soup and milk and watercress into the blender.

"You could have fooled me." Dr. Milgrim smacked her lips. "It tastes as if it had been simmering for hours." Her beady eyes darted toward Mariah. "One day perhaps Mariah could start the supper. That would make life a little easier for you, Gertrude. More responsibility at home would be better for her than all those extracurricular activities of hers."

"I'm finished with all that," Mariah announced. "I ended my club today."

"You what?" Mr. and Mrs. Delany said at once. Even Irwin's spoon clattered to his bowl.

"What was it this time? Author-of-the-Month?" Dr. Milgrim said. "What an idea. I've heard of Fruit-of-the-Month, and Book-of-the-Month, but you eat the fruit and keep the book. What on earth do you do with an author?"

"An author came to talk to our club once a month," Mariah explained.

"Really?" Dr. Milgrim looked dubious.

"And it was the best success I ever had," Mariah cried with more feeling that she intended. "I had calls from authors as far away as Rapid City. I had vice presidents. I had my assistant principal asking if she could come. I had a national magazine here to write about us. This afternoon I had the l-legendary T. M. Obermeyer . . ." At this point Mariah heard her voice quiver and climb. Suddenly she remembered the angry, scrunched-up face of T. M. Obermeyer. She could hear her dry, cold voice wrecking not only her club, but her love of the Fanny Frost books. Tears, large and sloppy, actually began to spill down her cheeks. Her voice caught. She couldn't speak.

The doorbell rang.

"Mariah, dear." Mrs. Delany leaned toward her, her face full of concern.

"I really want to go do my homework and my science project," Mariah managed in a sputtering, hold-back-my-tears voice.

The doorbell rang again.

"That's funny," Mr. Delany said, pushing back his chair. "Are we expecting anyone, Gertrude?"

"Not that I know of."

The bell rang again as he went to answer it.

"My schoolwork is my first priority," Mariah

continued, even though she had begun to sob. But no one was listening anymore. They were trying to hear what someone was saying to Mr. Delany at the front door. In a minute, Mr. Delany returned to the dining room. A few paces behind him was a short, red-faced man in a plaid lumberjacket, with a bulging knapsack and a bedroll on his back. He held a stuffed duffel bag in one hand.

"Hello, there," the man greeted them. "I'm sure looking forward to the next thirty days in New York. It's like a dream come true to be back here. Ms. Mariah Delany, you are my fairy godmother." He stepped up to Dr. Milgrim and took her hand in his. He shook her hand vigorously. "It's May the third and I'm Don Cowper, your author of the month."

Mariah could never quite remember what happened next, nor did she really want to.

14

Actually, like it or not, Mariah would never forget the way her mother's face turned a mushroom color, or the way Dr. Milgrim reared back from Don Cowper's handshake, or the way Irwin began to crack all his knuckles at once as her father fell back into his chair in surprise.

"Your little club has given this writer one big lift." Don Cowper contined to pump Dr. Milgrim's trapped hand. "I was blocked from here to Kalamazoo. Haven't finished a sentence in three years, and then just talking to you on the phone turned me around. I realized I was a writer after all. Somebody appreciated my work. Why, I wrote a whole rough draft on the bus, *The Revenge of the Planet of the Plants*. I think it could be a winner. Bless your heart."

"I am not Mariah Delany," Dr. Milgrim said. "That" — she pointed to Mariah — "is the person you seek."

Now it was Don Cowper's turn to fall silent. In fact, as he gazed at Mariah, the room seemed to freeze.

"You thought Mariah was a grown-up?" Irwin said.

Don Cowper nodded slowly.

An odd choking sound came from Irwin, as if he didn't want it to but couldn't help it. "Oh, boy." He gasped. "You thought 'author of the month' meant you could stay here for a month?"

"Ten days, anyway," Don Cowper said sadly. "A week maybe?"

"Did you discuss this with Mariah?" Mr. Delany asked, looking at Mariah.

"I called her long distance after I got her letter. The connection wasn't too good. I guess I was excited. I told her I'd like to accept her invitation to speak to her club. It would help sell my books. Why, it could even help get some of them back in print. I brought copies with me. I'd sell at a discount. I'd see New York again. I'd do research for my new book at the Forty-second Street library."

"Do sit down." Mrs. Delany uttered her first words. "Irwin, pull up a chair for our guest."

Irwin pulled up a chair as best he could, given that his shoulders were shaking and he was gasping for breath. He was laughing so hard he could scarcely stand.

"Irwin Delany," Mrs. Delany reprimanded him, only to realize in the next moment that her boss, Dr. Milgrim, was making the same noises as Irwin. Air was escaping from her nose in short snorts.

She and Irwin pounded the table and jabbed at each other with each new burst of laughter.

Mr. and Mrs. Delany watched them in amazement and then, without warning, joined in. Mariah guessed it was true that with some people laughter was very contagious.

Her eyes and Don Cowper's met in a long, serious stare.

"I didn't know you were a kid," he said, "or I never would have come to stay."

"I didn't know you were coming to stay," Mariah said, "or I never would have asked you. I was going to call and tell you I've just ended my club."

Don Cowper sighed and looked at the chair Irwin had pulled up for him. His face was bleak. "I guess I better catch the next bus back. Sorry for the" — he looked at the Delanys — "mistake and inconvenience."

"But you mustn't go," Mr. Delany said, wiping his eyes and extending his hand. "Not after this."

"I have to get back to the bus terminal." He looked at his wristwatch. "I can't afford to stay in New York."

"Certainly you will spend the night here after coming such a long distance. We wouldn't hear of your leaving now. You can make your travel arrangements in the morning."

"I wouldn't want to be an inconvenience." Don Cowper glanced quickly into the living room at the sofa and the heaps of books spilling around it.

"No inconvenience at all. I'm sure Mariah would be happy to let you use her room." Mrs. Delany smiled. "She can bunk on the spare bed in my study."

The spare bed? It was a cot. Study? It was a cubbyhole with a slatted door. Her room was her sanctuary. Her safe place. But Mariah kept silent. There wasn't anything she could say.

Irwin was setting a place for Don Cowper. Mrs. Delany was spooning Hasty Soup and Rapid Stew into bowls for him. Mr. Delany was handing him a glass of wine.

Don Cowper tucked a napkin under his chin and drew up his chair. "Very delicious," he said of the Hasty Soup, but after he tasted his Rapid Stew he smacked his lips. "This reminds me of a dish I used to eat when I was at the University of Texas," he said.

"The University of Texas?" Mr. and Mrs. Delany cried together. It was where they had met. It turned out Don Cowper had graduated just a few years after the Delanys.

"I was a theater major," Don Cowper said. "When I lived in New York, I tried to support myself as an actor. When that didn't work, I began to teach. I taught junior high school in Brooklyn for a few years, and then I went out to Rapid City to teach on an Indian reservation. I began to write books while I was living in New York. Now I'm taking off a year, just to write."

Don Cowper told them stories about life on the reservation. He opened his knapsack and showed them some of the Indian crafts he had brought along. There was a hatband woven of horsehair and a baseball cap decorated with intricate beadwork.

Mariah sat watching her parents and Dr. Milgrim and Irwin listening intently to Don Cowper's stories. She observed the scene as if she were in a movie house viewing a film. They seemed to have forgotten all about her. They were so excited about Don Cowper having gone to their school and knowing people they knew and his stories about the reservation, they didn't even ask her about her meeting with T. M. Obermeyer.

Finally, Mr. Delany noticed Mariah's silence. "Mariah, how was that meeting you had today?"

"I'd rather not say." Mariah stared glumly at her plate.

"I see," Mr. Delany said kindly. "When you're ready to tell us, we'd like to hear."

Nobody even asked why she'd rather not say.

Mrs. Delany brought in coffee and dessert. There were more stories about Texas and college days, and then it was time for Dr. Milgrim to leave. She didn't want to go.

"I'm afraid I'll miss something," she said. "I've

had such a good time. All thanks to Mariah Delany and her club."

"And my misunderstanding," Don Cowper added, laughing. "I thought T. M. Obermeyer finished her *month* today, and I would begin my month on the day she left. Even though I'll only have one night in New York, it's been a good one."

"Why don't you stay for a few days at least?" Mr. Delany said. "That way, you could work at the library and perhaps Mariah could change her mind and schedule another meeting of her club."

A few more days? Another meeting? Mariah thought she'd scream.

Don Cowper looked at her. He seemed to understand something. "Tomorrow I'll see if I can reach an old neighbor in Brooklyn. Perhaps he'll have room for me to stay. That would give me the extra time I need."

"Oh, yes." Mariah felt tears of gratitude well up. Would it give her the time she needed? Or was it too late for that?

15

When she woke up in the morning, Mariah didn't want to leave the cot in the cubby. She didn't want to go to school, but once she got to school she didn't want to go home. What would she do there? Would Don Cowper be asleep in her bed, as he had been when she left? All day she avoided her friends. How could she tell them about Don Cowper? How could she explain about the meeting? Would she have to hold another one? She walked home slowly. There was no place else to go.

Mariah let herself into the apartment without making a sound. On the hall table there were two notes and a special delivery package. They were all for her.

The first note was from Don Cowper. "Off to the library," it read. The second was from Mrs. Levine. "We're not going to run the article on Obermeyer after all. It didn't work out the way we'd hoped." The package was a book. *Fanny Frost.* Book One. Mariah opened it, almost expecting something unpleasant to pop out. On the title page there was a handwritten inscription:

To Mariah Delany: You are a plucky, resourceful young person who tells the truth. Just the sort of reader I am proud to have. T.M.O.

Mariah read the inscription over and over, until it was memorized, until it seemed to be part of the book. But it wasn't part of the book, she reminded herself. It was separate. The author and the characters in a book were different, Mariah now realized, even though one could not exist without the other. She turned to Chapter One and began to read.

Something happened. Something more amazing than an author talking about her book, or signing it on the title page. Once again the magical world of Fanny Frost enveloped her. It was a world where ordinary life was lit by the impossible. Fanny Frost and the Picket children, learning that the sheep could speak and flying off on the back of an ewe to a place where no people had ever been before. Fanny Frost was so much better than T. M. Obermeyer. Fanny Frost was wonderful! Best of all, it was a book. A book Mariah could pick up and hold without having to extend an invitation or write a letter. It was a book that had started everything. Reading Willy Wild was what made Janice

Pike's visit special. It was Outlaw Joe that made everybody want to meet Joe Butts. It was Fanny Frost that had made Mariah try so hard to have T. M. Obermeyer speak to her club. Fanny Frost was a welcome guest in Mariah's house anytime. T. M. Obermeyer was a different story. Suddenly, Mariah's nose began to quiver. Her green eyes narrowed. Her lips became a thin line, even as she grinned.

She was having a brainstorm. She was having her best idea ever. She was going to tell Josie and Emma and Leah and Suzy and Dave. But halfway to the phone she stopped herself. This brainstorm would have to wait. There were things waiting for her on her desk. First things first.

Carefully, Mariah set her knapsack down on her bed. If she heard the door open, she would have plenty of time to grab her papers and run. She looked over at her desk and the waiting pile of homework assignments stacked on it. Sticking out from beneath the pile she saw the edge of her science folder. The sight of it made her stomach knot. It was time to water the begonia, but it seemed to her that the plant was beyond help. Even its leaves were shedding. "You are a plucky, resourceful young person," T. M. Obermeyer had written. Mariah pulled a chair up to her desk. Plucky, resourceful people figured out ways to manage.

*   *   *

Mariah managed to complete three assignments and not hear the front door open until it was too late.

"Hey, sorry," Don Cowper said. He stood in the doorway with an armload of books. "I'll just get some notepaper and take off."

"Where to?" Mariah asked.

"I could work in the living room till your folks come home. I've got everything I need for my *Planet of the Plants* book." He seemed excited. "The library had all these incredible works. They try to document how plants have complex ways of communicating and may respond to an emotional as well as a physical climate."

Mariah looked at her begonia and grimaced.

Don Cowper looked at it, too. "Doesn't seem very happy," he commented.

Mariah sighed. "It's my Independent Science Project, 'Observing Plant Life,' which I was supposed to be working on all term. It's due in five days. If I don't have it done I'll fail the term."

"Tell me more." Don Cowper sat down on her bed.

"I was supposed to set up a problem, assemble material, chart my observations, and draw a conclusion. I haven't set up anything, and all I've observed is that my plant is dying on me. It's miserable."

"Like you." Don Cowper nodded.

Mariah opened her folder. "I don't get it," she said. "It's had the same light and water, only back here" — she pointed to the day in April when she heard that T. M. Obermeyer would be her guest — "it was blooming with actual flowers. And here" — she pointed to yesterday, when T. M. Obermeyer ruined her club — "the flowers began to fall off."

Don Cowper took the folder from Mariah's hand. "This is very interesting. There is something very interesting here."

"There is?"

"It may seem farfetched, but I think that, without knowing it, you did set up a problem."

"I did?"

"Let me leave you some of the books I've been reading about how plants may respond to an emotional climate around them."

"Emotional?" Mariah asked.

"Feelings."

"You mean . . ." She began to see it. "When I've been feeling happy, my plant . . ."

He nodded.

"And when I'm miserable, my plant . . ."

"Right now I think you need these books more than I do." Don Cowper stood up, leaving the library books on the bed. "I'll work on my plot till dinner. You have a lot to do, Mariah." He picked up his notebook and pencils and started for the door. Then he turned. "About the meeting of your club . . . why don't you call it off? Along with all your schoolwork, it seems to me it's more than you can handle."

"I can too handle it," Mariah said.

"Mariah, this club idea of yours is a good one, but it takes a lot of work."

"I CAN TOO HANDLE IT," Mariah repeated. "You are my next guest, and everybody in school will know it because this meeting will be bigger and better than any of the others. Also, it will be the last."

"Mariah — " he began.

"No ifs, ands, or buts." She turned to the pile of books he had left for her. "Now please close the door behind you. I've got a ton of work."

16

"This is the oddest experiment I ever heard of." Mrs. Demot shook her head over Mariah's work. "But you *did* set up a problem, even if it was after and not before the observation. You certainly have made something of a point. I can't criticize your charts or your reading." She seemed to reflect as she shuffled through Mariah's notes and papers. "You have even drawn some lessons that are beyond the scientific and are related to your own behavior over these last few months." There was another pause and then she turned to look at Mariah. "Yes, I will accept this work."

It was as if a medium-sized stone had been lifted off Mariah's heart. Her project — "Do Plants Reflect the Emotional Climate Around Them?" — had charted the little begonia's rise and fall along with her own. She had documented in detail the events of her life and those of the plant. She had noted the amazing similarity in their fates. Even though the begonia had received the same amount of water and light and had not changed its soil condition, its health seemed to fluctuate with

Mariah's moods and feelings. As of that very morning, on the completion of her project, the begonia showed strong signs of improvement.

"Now there's something else," Mariah said.

"Something else?" Mrs. Demot smiled. "Have you done *two* science projects, Mariah?"

"I want permission to hold my last Author-of-the-Month Club meeting, featuring the author Don Cowper, at a Friday assembly. That way, the whole school can hear him."

"Your *last* meeting?" Mrs. Demot smiled. "I don't think there will be a problem."

The final Friday assembly of the year, featuring Don Cowper as the guest, was a great success. He showed some magic tricks. He made a quarter turn into two dimes and a nickel. He made one rubber ball turn into ten. He pulled colored scarves out of a hat. "I love to do magic tricks, and I love to write books," he said. "They both have to appear easy, which takes hard work. My books are about adventures in outer space, but I've had an adventure right here on earth that was a doozie." He peered out at the audience till he saw Mariah. "I received a letter from a stranger with a great idea. The idea was the Mariah Delany Author-of-the-Month Club. Because of Mariah's club I learned that a reader is a real person and not what I expected. Mariah learned that a writer is a real person and not what she expected. We all came together because of a book. Books make things happen. In this case, books and Mariah Delany. Thank you, Mariah."

Everyone turned to look at Mariah, and Don Cowper began to clap his hands. Soon everyone was applauding, and Mrs. Demot gestured to Mariah that she should stand up. A few of her classmates began to holler, "Speech!"

Mariah smiled. "Thanks."

"You can't close the club down," Dave called out. "It's a success!"

"If you liked this club," Mariah told the audience, "you'll LOVE my next one."

Mrs. Demot and Mr. Terril rolled their eyes to the ceiling. Mariah was sure she even heard one of them groan, but she wasn't going to pass up an opportunity like this to unveil her new idea.

"What's the next one?" the audience asked.

"Watch for the posters," Mariah said mysteriously. In her mind's eye she could see the poster announcing the Mariah Delany READ-AND-TALK-ABOUT-A-BOOK-CLUB.

The first book would be *Fanny Frost*, Book One. They would all read it, and then they would get together at her house and talk about it. Maybe they would do sections out loud or even take the parts of the different characters like a play. This club couldn't fail. The idea was so simple. No flea markets. No tap dances. No diguises. No surprises, except the ones found between the covers of . . . a book.